THE UNICORN THIEF

UNICORNS OF THE MIST

THE UNICORN THIEF

UNICORNS OF THE MIST

R.R. RUSSELL

Published by Sourcebooks Jabberwocky, an imprint of Sourcebooks, Inc.
P.O. Box 4410, Naperville, Illinois 60567-4410
(630) 961-3900
Fax: (630) 961-2168
www.jabberwockykids.com

Library of Congress Cataloging-in-Publication data is on file with the publisher.

Source of Production: Worzalla, Stevens Point, WI, USA
Date of Production: March 2014
Run Number: 5000978

Printed and bound in the United States of America.
WOZ 10 9 8 7 6 5 4 3 2 1

For Isaac

Chapter 1

THE UNICORN'S NOSTRILS FLARED at the thief in warning. Her breath came out in puffs of outrage, a visible vapor in the crisp night air. The mare's deadly horn glinted in the light of the lantern, but the thief stayed calm. He held out his hand, palm down. Then he took the tiny instrument from his pocket, held it to his lips, and began to play.

The flattened ears perked up and turned toward the sound. He'd practiced this song, refined it even more, he believed, than the great Darian ever had. His fingers danced over the holes as he blew, making music to lull the powerful Night Spark. To bring her completely under his control.

Darian, the great herder, was a man of many secrets, and this was one of them. The thief's throat tightened around his song, his heart caught in the clench of regret. Would Westland ever see Darian again? Would he? It was too easy to succumb to such dark thoughts anywhere on castle grounds, but especially here, in the royal stables.

The thief fitted Night Spark with a halter and led her out of the stall. He could hear the boots of the guards on the cobblestone outside, pacing in a steady, serious rhythm. Alert, strong. Nothing but the queen's best to guard her best.

Those guards would have a hard time explaining this. It was too bad, but it had to be done. The thief guided Night Spark through the secret opening in the back wall of the stable and into the shaft of darkness—Darian's passageway. Night Spark shuffled, eyelids drooping, as though she were sleepwalking. The thief slid the hidden panel shut and disappeared with the unicorn into the underground maze.

• • •

Twig bent to put the last plate in the dishwasher, and Ben scooped a blob of frosting off it. He licked his finger. Twig made a face. She picked up the box of detergent and showed Ben how to open it.

Ben sniffed the citrusy detergent scent—too hard. He sneezed, and his shaggy brown hair flew into his eyes.

"I still don't understand," Ben said between sneezes. "How does this stuff get the dishes clean?"

Twig grinned. "Watch." She poured the detergent into the dishwasher, then shut the door and turned the dial. Ben's eyes widened. He knelt down, ear to the dishwasher door.

"Water!"

Ben had been raised in another world—Terracornus, land of the unicorns. He'd spent much of his life here on Lonehorn Island, in the Earth Land, as he called it, but he'd never seen modern technology. Until the Murleys had come to Lonehorn Island and built Island Ranch—a home, pony ranch, and informal school for six troubled girls—the island had been abandoned.

"It's a machine with a motor, like the truck, only it runs on electricity. The same stuff that powers the lights in here."

"It pumps water over the dishes?"

"I guess so. It sprays them."

Ben listened for a moment, then threw open the door to the cupboard under the sink, an eager, searching look in his brown eyes. "The water comes from under here."

Twig turned on the faucet. "It's all connected."

"Amazing."

He pulled on the dishwasher door, trying to open it, but the handle wasn't visible under the matching panel across the top of the machine, and he kept missing the spot.

Twig bit her lip. Should she ask him now? If not now, when? She couldn't wait any longer. In just a couple months, her dad would come and take her home, away from the island. "Ben?"

"Hm?"

Twig pressed in and pulled out, unlatching and opening the machine a crack for him.

He peeked inside. "It stopped," he muttered with a frown.

"I was thinking, since I explained something to you, maybe you could explain something to me."

"Sure." He closed the door and started turning the dial every which way. *Heavy wash, light wash, super soak, dry.* "It dries them too?"

Twig let out an exasperated breath and cranked the dial to the *off* position. She stood in front of the machine, blocking his view.

Ben rose, brow creased. "What?"

Twig took the note from her pocket. The one Ben had dropped back in Terracornus, before they'd killed Dagger, the bloodthirsty unicorn who'd led the island's herd to attack the ranch. Dagger had been determined to kill Twig's unicorn, Wonder, whom she'd raised from birth.

Ben had tried to hide the note from her, but in his haste, he'd dropped it, and she'd slipped it into her pocket. She hadn't had time to read it until they were safe back at the ranch. And then there'd been so much going on—finding out that Ben was a long-lost relative of the Murleys; Twig's thirteenth birthday, which she almost hadn't lived to see; Skyping her dad, who was in the army and deployed overseas, and talking to him for the first time in a year. It was hard to believe that was just yesterday. It was hard to believe that after all they'd done, their work wasn't over. It was only just beginning.

Twig pressed the note against her jeans, flattening the crumpled paper. She held it out. "What's going on, Ben?"

"How'd you get that?" Ben snatched it out of her hands and stuffed it in his own pocket.

"You dropped it. What does it mean?"

Ben crossed his arms over the too-big T-shirt he'd borrowed from Mr. Murley. "It's nothing. Nothing that I can do anything about."

"Merrill said—"

"Merrill's wrong."

"Fine. Merrill's wrong. You can still tell me what he meant. What's going on in Terracornus?"

"The same old problems."

Twig put on her best "Merrill" voice—gruff yet warm—and quoted his note. "'It's worse than I feared here. As soon as we've dealt with Dagger, you must come to Westland. For the sake of all unicorns, all Terracornus, you must appeal to the queen.' That's what it says. Sounds like more than the same old problems to me." Twig had the cryptic phrase, written by their friend and old herder, Merrill, memorized. A friend of Ben's father, Darian, Merrill had come to the island to help Twig learn to ride Wonder and to teach her to wield a short sword and handle a bow.

"But it *is* the same. There's always the threat of war in Terracornus. Merrill wants me to appeal to the queen to step down and put a democratic process back in place, so that Westland can be an example to all the other lands, instead of becoming more and more like them. He thinks Westland can be a reminder to all Terracornus of how things were meant to be."

"Can it?"

"It used to be." Abruptly, Ben's expression hardened. "But it doesn't matter. There's nothing I can do about it."

"Why does Merrill think you can then?"

"The queen knew my father well. He was the greatest herder in Westland, an important man. But she's changed. The herders have been disbanded. Everything's changed. I cannot influence the queen. Not now, not ever."

CHAPTER 2

BEN GATHERED UP THE books he'd just finished and carried the armful back to the bookshelf in the living room. He carefully slid each one back into place, then stood back and studied the shelves. So many books! So much he didn't know. After nearly a week at the ranch, he was beginning to wonder if he'd ever understand the way this world worked.

He began pulling out new titles, making another stack. The girls were all hunched over the table in the dining area behind him, working out something to do with numbers, every now and then peeking at him wistfully.

Except for Casey. The youngest of the girls and Twig's roommate, Casey was huddled in the little space between the end of the bookcase and the couch, her back to Ben, trying to hide the bundle of strange, blue-lined paper she was writing on. Casey loved to hear Ben's stories about Terracornus and about the unicorns of Lonehorn Island, and then she loved to retell them, making them even better every time. Yesterday, she'd been given an assignment to tell a story, this time on paper.

A tear fell on the pages as Casey flipped her wooden pencil around and jabbed at the writing with its rubbery end. It made a muddy-looking streak. Casey rubbed harder, and the paper tore. Ben moved to put a hand on her shoulder, then hesitated, torn between wanting to mind his own business and wanting to rescue her.

Casey's writing jumped out at Ben, so full of enthusiasm—and familiar characters—that he couldn't help reading.

The Grate Gators teeth shutted and he pulled por Joe down and down and the Soowamp bumbled up like a grate big buuuuurp! And that was the end off Joe. But it wasunt the end of the story! Ed lassowed Joe's unicorn Dancers tale and tyed her to his fathefull Thunder, and toled the prensess Margury to grab and hold on. Thunder pulled Dancer and Margury out off the mud and they rode together out off the Soowamp and that is how the brave Ed wun the byootifull prensess Margury in the ferst Deth Soowamp Dool.

Casey rubbed the back of her hand over her eyes and rose, clutching the stack of papers to her chest.

"All done?" Ben said.

Casey jumped, and the papers flew from her hands. She fumbled to catch them.

"Sorry." Ben scooped papers off the floor.

"Don't look! Please, Ben."

"Like he wants to look," Mandy said under her breath.

"Sorry. I already peeked at part of it. And of course I want to read it. It's good. And it *is* about the Death Swamp, after all."

He'd just told the girls that story last night, about how two rivals after the heart of one girl, Margery—not really a princess, but still—fought in the Death Swamp.

When Margery's suitors heard she'd wandered into the swamp, which few ever came out of alive, they'd each entered from opposite sides, vowing that whoever saved her and emerged with her would win the girl. Both were exceedingly clever, great riders of dauntless unicorns, and they managed to reach the middle of the swamp, where they found Margery sinking into the mud. The two had set aside their rivalry to try to save her, but Joe had been snapped up in the jaws of a swamp lizard.

Ed was faced with a terrible dilemma. Both Joe and Margery had only moments to live. According to legend, Joe had valiantly insisted that Ed save Margery. Just before being dragged into the black waters, he'd pulled out a handkerchief embroidered with the symbol of his herder division, tossed it to Ed, and said, "Give this to Margery, with my love."

Regina had sighed dreamily at that line, and Ben had wished he'd stuck with a battle story, or at least a story of one of the many Death Swamp Duels that had taken place ever since, usually to settle disputes over land or unicorns. Instead of coming out of the swamp with the girl and the handkerchiefs of their rivals, duelers now fought to capture their rivals' flags.

Maybe next time, he should just tell the story of the first Death Swamp Duel Casey's way and leave the romantic gesture out.

Casey hesitated at the blue plastic tray brimming with the girls' completed work, clutching her story and looking so small. Ben didn't know what to say. He wasn't used to being around a bunch of girls. He picked up a page that had drifted under the table.

Twig gave Mandy a threatening glare and joined Ben in helping Casey put the pages back in order.

"Everybody loves the stories you tell, Casey. I'm sure Mrs. Murley will love this one too."

"It's not the same when I have to *write* it! It's awful! I know it!"

Gently, Twig took the papers from Casey and placed them in the tray on the side table.

Casey sat down to work on her math with the other girls.

Janessa leaned over to Ben. "Thanks," she whispered. "She adores you, you know."

Ben blushed. He knew. She followed him and Twig everywhere. But while she looked at Twig with the trust of a sister,

Casey watched Ben expectantly. Like she was always ready to be impressed.

Mrs. Murley emerged from the kitchen, oblivious to the drama, and sat at the end of the table with the contents of the blue tray and a big cup of coffee.

All around the table, pencils stilled. Casey appeared to have stopped breathing. Mrs. Murley picked up Casey's story and began to read. The corner of Mrs. Murley's mouth twitched up in a smile. She held an arm out. "Come here, Casey."

With a sheepish smile, Casey obeyed. Mrs. Murley squeezed her against her side as she finished reading the story.

"This is wonderful, Casey. I knew you could do it."

The prick of tears came on so unexpectedly. Ben turned away. He felt like he'd been punched in his chest. He wanted to run far away from here, and at the same time, he wanted to stay, to be like Casey and to hear those words he'd never heard from a mother. *This is wonderful. I knew you could do it.*

You have to go back to Terracornus. You have to go back to the queen. Merrill kept saying it, and now he had Twig saying it too.

What was he supposed to do? Going back there would mean turning his back on the herd. If he went to the castle, he might never return to the island—and for what? To talk to a ruler who cared nothing for what a herder had to say?

"Ben?" Mr. Murley called from the entryway. He sounded out of breath.

Ben ran to the front door.

Mr. Murley stood in the doorway, boots on, face flushed under the hood of his jacket. Under the cover of the porch, he pushed the hood back, and rainwater spilled over his shoulders. "It's Indy."

CHAPTER 3

"WHAT'S WRONG?" BEN SAID.

A stampede of girls filled the entryway behind him.

"Indy's getting restless out there," Mr. Murley said. "I could use your help calming him down."

Twig reached for her red jacket—the one she liked to zip up like a turtle shell.

"Hold on, Twig." Mrs. Murley came up behind the girls. "David, do you need Twig out there?"

"I think Ben and I can handle it."

Twig scrunched her face up. "What about Wonder?"

"She's a little upset, but she'll be fine once Indy's under control," Mr. Murley said.

Ben bit back a laugh at the thought of Indy under control. He turned to put on his boots, but something thwacked the side of his head. A sock.

"Hey!" Ben pivoted around to face the girls. Twig's blue eyes gleamed with triumph at her victory.

"What are you smiling about, Ben?" Regina, the oldest after Twig, narrowed her dark eyes at Ben.

"Yeah, it's not funny that Twig can't go," added Casey, with those big brown eyes. Eyes that had searched the woods for him long before that desperate, awful night when he'd come to hide a unicorn here on the ranch. She'd known he was out there, even when he wasn't supposed to exist.

"I wasn't laughing at Twig," Ben said.

"Yeah, right." Mandy tilted her head of blond curls at him skeptically. Her usual scowl deepened.

"You're already behind, Twig," Mrs. Murley said. "Just get that work done, and you can go see Wonder."

Twig glowered at Ben and flung her jacket aside. She muttered something about it not being fair and fixed her eyes on the rain-streaked window.

Ben picked up the jacket and handed it to Twig over her shoulder. Mesmerized by the rain, lost in thought, she made no move to take it. He gave her pale braid a little tug, and she glanced back at him.

"Sorry. I wish you could come. I wish we could ride."

He wished so many things that couldn't all be, at least not at the same time.

Ben grabbed his cape and hurried into his boots. Poor Twig. But even worse was Indy, shut up in the stable. His unicorn stallion didn't know what to make of this place. He was used to running free on this island, the home of the Earth Land's only unicorns, the last free herd of unicorns in any world.

Ben had spent the whole morning indoors—a unicorn rider, buried in books, captivated by the world within those bright yellow ranch house walls. The warmth, the contraptions, the people—people who cared to know where he was, what he was doing. Oh, they tried to give him his space. They weren't the same with him as they were with each other. But still…

He was so used to being on his own since his father died. And before that—being with Father had been like being on his own, only without the loneliness. They had known each other so well. They'd worked together as unicorn herders for most of Ben's life. Sometimes Ben wondered who he was without Father.

He didn't know the answer yet, but one thing was for sure—he was a herder and Indy's rider. Foul weather or not, he belonged in the woods with his unicorn, breathing in the wild, cold fragrance of cedar and rain, not cinnamon French toast, hot coffee, and lemony spray cleaner.

He hurried outside and jumped down the porch steps and over a row of daffodils bent low with the heaviness of the spring rain. He darted to the stables, where Mr. Murley already had the door open.

The stable was alive with the distressed wails of the more skittish ponies. Others nickered attempts to make peace with the fearsome Indy, who was locked in the back stall with his daughter, Wonder. All along the stable aisle, the ponies—one for each of the six girls—tossed their heads in agitation. Over the stall wall, Mrs. Murley's horse, Feather, bared her teeth at Indy. Indy's horn ripped through the air. Feather backed away, neighing her remorse.

Sparkler, the alpha mare, neighed threateningly at Indy, a fearless—and foolish—attempt to come to Feather's defense. Wonder leaped and rammed the stall with her horn. Ben jumped back. The ponies cried wildly as the young unicorn took her father's side against the stable full of animals she'd grown up with. Ben's heart thudded in his chest and rain pelted the skylights overhead, adding a fierce, angry rhythm to the stable sounds.

"Indy," Ben said firmly, reassuringly, "I'm coming. Stand down now, the both of you."

Indy's low growl-snort answered him. A smaller whirl of white mane swished next to Indy's majestic head. The long, gleaming spiral of Indy's horn with its midnight-blue stripe streaked back and forth above the stable walls in a pantomime of battle. Ben knew how well-trained and disciplined his unicorn actually was. He was merely mimicking fighting his way out. He was powerful enough to thrust his horn right through the stall walls until they were nothing but a pile of splinters.

Indy wouldn't do it, especially with Ben there. But would

Wonder? Sparkler reared, and again Wonder rammed the stall. There was a slam-crack. Wonder was young, impulsive, not as disciplined as Indy, and her rider wasn't here. Rain Cloud called for Sparkler to lay off, and Indy gave Wonder a poke with his horn, but his heart wasn't in it. He shot Ben a defiant glare as if to say, *I won't break out of here, and I won't charge at that impertinent pony, but if Wonder wants to do it, why should I stop her?*

"Ben?" Mr. Murley couldn't quite hide the tremor in his voice.

"Get Twig, Mr. M. Quick."

Wonder backed up. She bent her knees. Ben knew that look. She wasn't going to charge this time; she was going to jump. Right out of her stall and into Sparkler's. The pony wouldn't stand a chance.

"Wonder!" Ben said firmly.

The feet came down, still in her own stall. Wonder hadn't jumped quite high enough. But was it just because Ben had distracted her? Could she really jump out of the stall? She never had before, but she seemed to amaze them with some new feat almost every day.

Ben hurried to open Sparkler's stall. The frightened pony rushed out. Before he could get hold of her to take her outside, there was a flash of white mane and flying hooves. Ben jumped back and plastered himself against the stalls at the side of the aisle.

"Stop right there!"

Hooves skidded on the dirt floor of the aisle, sending stray bits of wood shavings flying.

Twig was there, soaking wet, jacketless, and in stocking feet. She grasped Sparkler's halter in one hand and held her other palm out, the picture of calm determination and authority. "Just what do you think you're doing, Wonder?"

Wonder dipped her head and neighed her appeal to her rider. Mrs. Murley ran in and took Sparkler from Twig. Mr. Murley was right behind her.

Twig caught a handful of Wonder's mane, then slipped her arms around her neck.

Ben let out a breath of relief and strode to the stall the two unicorns shared. Though they were solidly built, the walls rumbled with Indy's angry movements.

"There, now. I'm here."

Indy pawed the ground and fixed Ben with a fierce stare. And Ben saw, not anger anymore, but fear and yearning, barely contained by the stallion's dignity. Mr. Murley stayed back a few paces behind Ben in the aisle, quiet and still, just in case Ben needed him.

"I'll get this troublemaker out of here." Mrs. Murley snapped a lead on Sparkler's halter and took her outside.

As Ben opened the stall door, Indy gave the air one last slash with his horn, just to show Ben he really meant it.

Behind him, Ben sensed Mr. Murley jolt and move closer.

"It's okay," Ben told his uncle before he could jump in front of him and upset Indy all over again. "Indy, stand down."

Indy bowed his head, though he sent Ben a sideways look of contempt with his eyes, the dark, liquid silver color of all unicorns. Ben stroked Indy's neck. "It's just the rain, Indy-boy. I know it sounds strange."

The island wind attacked the glass with a heavier pelting, trying to batter its way in. Or to drive Indy out, where he belonged. Indy neighed, ears pinned back.

"Ah, Indy. You're right. I'm sorry. Your island wants you, and you want your island." Ben stroked Indy's neck, and Wonder jumped in a circle around Twig, showing her own younger, fresher brand of impatience. "You too, Wonder. Outside with both of you. Sparkler can come back in and calm down where she feels more comfortable."

The ponies nickered their agreement, and Wonder nuzzled Ben's side.

Mr. Murley glanced at the skylights, at the downpour pounding the glass.

"They'll be all right," Twig said. "They can handle a little rain."

Mr. Murley did what he could to help turn the unicorns out. Which mostly meant staying out of their way and opening the paddock gates.

Twig ran back to the house to get her jacket and to get

Mandy to help her calm Sparkler. Ben had a little talk with Indy about staying in the pasture and making sure Wonder did too. Indy and Wonder were expert jumpers, a combination of natural ability and the training Ben and Twig had put them through. They could leap the fence and disappear into the woods if they wanted to. But both creatures were loyal to their riders, and Wonder would follow Indy's lead.

The unicorns leaped in the rain. They kicked up mud and turf, delighting in the fresh, wet air. Mr. Murley stood at the pasture gate, watching them. David Murley was the great-grand nephew of Edward Murley, an early settler in Washington state, and the first Earth Lander to settle—or try to settle—on Lonehorn Island. Edward Murley was Ben's great-great-grandfather.

Edward's sons had disappeared into Terracornus through the island's hidden passage. As far as Ben knew, they were the first Earth Landers to settle in Terracornus in hundreds of years. The original unicorn herders had taken the last, endangered unicorns from the Earth Land to the newly discovered, empty world they named Terracornus. They had to protect the magnificent creatures from people who hunted them for their supposedly magical horns.

Much later, when Terracornus had become dangerous, no longer the sanctuary it once was, a few unicorns had been let back into the Earth Land through the island's passage. Ben's great-grandfather, Elijah Murley, had taken on the duty of keeping watch over Lonehorn Island's small herd—the last *free* herd in any world.

"Indy cannot stay here, Mr. M." As much as he liked him, Ben didn't feel right calling a man he'd just met *uncle*, and just plain *David* seemed disrespectful, so he'd adopted Janessa's name for him. "Indy cannot handle being fenced in."

Mr. Murley nodded at the woods surrounding the ranch. Cedars and firs, thick ferns and mosses growing in their shadows. Tangles of brambles taking over any spot where the sun dared to peek through.

"It's cold and wet out there, Ben. When it doesn't rain, there's the fog. We've had some sunny days, but summer's still a long way off."

"But it's still home." Not the ranch. Not Terracornus. Not anymore. He belonged in Lonehorn Island's misty woods with the herd his father had raised him to protect. "It stays dry in our hollow, mostly."

"What about the herd? Is Indy safe out there with them?"

As if in answer, the distant call of a unicorn sounded. Plaintive, searching. Possibly injured.

The herd would be looking for a new leader now that Dagger was dead. It was Ben's job to make sure they ended up with a better one.

Yesterday, he and Twig had planted trails of apples and

carrots in the woods, leading to bins of feed. Normally, he wouldn't feed wild animals. It was best for them to graze naturally, and there was plenty for them to eat now that spring was here. But with Dagger, these unicorns had begun to hunt, killing rabbits and raccoons. They'd become more predatory the more they killed. He wanted to make sure they were too full of oats to continue down that deadly path—and that they were as content as possible when he and Twig began to approach them.

"I'm not sure. Some of them are hurt, and we might be able to help. It's time to think about the unicorns and what they need."

Mr. Murley nodded thoughtfully. "But what about you, Ben? What do you need?"

Ben opened his mouth, but no words came out.

"How would you like a room of your own? I could add one, on the back side of the house."

A room of his own! Ben had watched the ranch being built. He'd spent countless hours staring at the place from the cover of the brush at the edge of the clearing, wondering what it was like inside. The thought of living here permanently…

He didn't want to go back to Terracornus. He wouldn't, no matter how many messages Merrill sent. But staying at the ranch would make the Murleys guardians of sorts. They'd feel even more responsible for him.

And Ben had learned something about this world—the Earth Land—that he'd never understood before. They expected different things—lesser things—from their youth. Above all they wanted them to be safe, where above all Ben's father, Darian, had wanted him to be honorable and brave.

Ben twisted a fold of his cape in his hand. Rain washed over his red-cold knuckles. His father's violent death gave Ben respect for the values of this world. So did the depth of the Murleys' love for each one of their girls. But he didn't know how to live like that. How to be *Ben* like that.

"I need to be out there, with the herd. I thank you for everything, Mr. M, but I just cannot stay."

Sadness, then acceptance glimmered in Mr. Murley's eyes.

"Twig's a herder now too. She—"

Already Mr. Murley was shaking his head. "Twig has to stay here. She's our responsibility. As long as she gets her schoolwork and her chores done, she can help you. But this is her home right now."

"I understand," Ben said.

But he didn't like it, not one bit. She was a herder at heart, just like him; he knew it. And soon her father would come back from that war he was fighting in a far-off desert land. He'd take her home with him, away from the Murleys. Ben understood that the Murleys wanted this time with her, but shouldn't she be allowed to spend what little time she had left on Lonehorn Island leaping through the mist, being a herder and Wonder's rider?

Twig was right. It wasn't fair. She'd never fully know the life of a herder. The life she was meant for.

CHAPTER 4

TWIG CLOSED HER HISTORY book and put her paper in the pile for Mrs. Murley to check. The ranch was still soggy outside from yesterday's rain, but the downpour had ended. She hurried outside, headed for the paddocks. She'd say hello to her pony, Rain Cloud, first. He was turned out in the paddock closest to the stable, with the other ponies and Feather. Then she'd go to Wonder, in the far paddock with Indy. Ben had been outside since dawn, keeping a close eye on the unicorns, making sure there wasn't any more trouble between them and the ponies.

Fresh air filled her lungs, and mist dampened her cheeks. She contemplated which to do next—archery practice, ride Wonder, ride Rain Cloud…but the sight on the front lawn stopped her short. Mr. Murley and Ben were wrestling with a tangle of poles and a mass of blue fabric. A tent.

"Okay," Mr. Murley said. "Go!"

Tent poles in their hands, both of them stepped back and pushed up. The tent sprang to life. Ben let go, and the tent pulled one of the stakes free of the earth and teetered off the ground.

Twig jogged over. "What are you guys doing?"

Mr. Murley rubbed his muddy palms on his jeans. "I think we worked out a compromise, Twig."

"About where I'm going to live," Ben said.

Ben had reluctantly taken Mr. Murley to see the shelter he lived in, little more than a bunch of evergreen branches leaned against a tree in the hollow, a small, hidden clearing under a canopy of trees. Mr. Murley had *not* been impressed.

Ben picked up the mallet and gave the stake another whack. He scrambled into the tent as though he couldn't wait a moment longer. He paced around inside the tent, then crossed his arms and gave a satisfied nod, trying to regain his characteristic calm air. Lately Twig wondered if he was as surprised as she was by the different side of himself these new discoveries brought out—amazed, intrigued, almost exuberant.

"Look!" He worked the zipper around the tent door, back and forth.

Twig ducked inside the tent with him.

"Mr. M says I can sleep in here," Ben said.

"In the yard?"

"No, in the hollow. In my usual spot. Just in this tent."

From the other side of the tent wall, Mr. Murley said, "I don't know if you can set it up yourself, though. It really does take two. Maybe I should go into town and pick up a smaller one."

Ben exited the tent. "Twig can help me."

"Of course," Mr. Murley said. But he looked nervous.

"I wouldn't want the rest of you coming out there into the woods, upsetting the herd. But Twig can ride Wonder out there with me and help me with the tent."

"And help him get things going with the herd," she said hopefully.

Mr. Murley frowned. "What are you two getting at?"

"Can she not stay with me, just for a few nights?"

Twig's heart fluttered at the thought of spending the night in the hollow, with just a wall of vinyl between her and her unicorn. Like a real herder.

"Mrs. Murley and I will have to discuss it."

Twig threw her arms around Mr. Murley. Mrs. Murley would say yes. She had to.

•••

Casey helped Twig into the big, framed backpack. It was filled with clothes and food, and a sleeping bag was strapped to the top. She hadn't been camping since before Mom and Daddy split up, when she was just a kindergartner. But the tent and other supplies were secured on Ben's and Indy's backs, and they knew what to do. The wooded depths of Lonehorn Island had been their home for years.

Wonder bounced around the pasture. She had never spent the night in the woods either—not to sleep anyway. Twig had sneaked out with her many nights to train for battle against Dagger and the herd, but that was different.

Wonder had been born in the ranch's stable. A little white moonbeam of hope entering the world on a night of sadness and terror. A night that had taken both Wonder's mother, Wind Catcher, and Ben's father, Darian. Dagger had killed them in a frenzy over Indy, his rival, and also over the herders standing between him and his prey—the animals of Island Ranch.

The girls of Island Ranch stood solemnly, all in a row.

"We have something for you, Ben. Twig already gave you a Bible, so…" Taylor gestured for Janessa, and she stepped forward and pulled a book out from behind her back.

A wonderfully fat book filled with diagrams of tools and machines. He opened it, and his eyes got big and hungry. He smiled at the girls. "Thanks."

"I'll be back for chores on Monday morning," Twig promised.

Taylor took Casey's hand in hers. "We'll take care of Rain Cloud."

Casey broke away and threw her arms around Twig.

"It's just for two nights," Twig said.

Casey looked into Twig's eyes with an expression Twig

had seen before, one that pierced her heart every time. "Come back, Twig."

"I will," Twig promised, just like last time.

One day, while they were grooming their ponies side by side, Casey had told Twig her mom had promised to come back, but she never did. That was how she ended up here.

The familiar route to the hollow felt different this time. The ride was jerkier, with the unicorns carrying such awkward burdens. It was strange to travel this path in the daylight, without sneaking, without fear of getting caught. But then, why did she have a knot in her gut?

Twig had daydreamed about being a herder like Ben, keeping the unicorns of Lonehorn Island safe from discovery and from each other. Now she had her chance. What if she couldn't do it? What if Ben realized she wasn't really who he'd thought she could be? Maybe she shouldn't be trying to do this at all. Soon she'd have to leave and go back to her dad and her stepfamily. Would she still be the new Twig then? Away from Wonder? Away from the island, where everything had changed?

CHAPTER 5

EN LOOKED AT HIS hollow, filled up with the bright blue tent. It was amazing, all the things people in the Earth Land had made. But now that he'd brought a piece of that world here, it just didn't feel right. He shut his eyes, overcome with longing for a time when the only things that could really fill this hollow were a crackling fire and the sound of his father's voice, rising and falling with the stories he loved to tell.

Casey would've loved Darian. He had lots of harrowing stories about the Death Swamp. Who would have thought he'd survive three trips through that swamp, only to die here, on his beloved, beautiful island—attacked by the unicorn he'd once loved?

"Ben? Are you okay?"

He blinked at Twig. "Sure."

She grabbed one of their bags, unzipped it, and began to paw through the frozen, icelike plastic things and colorful containers. "Mrs. Murley packed us turkey salad sandwiches. And…" She grinned big and whipped out a long, flat container.

"Peanut butter cookies with chocolate chips! Just wait till you try them."

They ate a quick lunch, and Ben had to agree the cookies were amazing—chewy with a pleasing crunch of sprinkled sugar on top. Then it was time to get to work with the herd.

Ben brushed the crumbs off his hands and fumbled with the lid to the cookie container. "The first thing is to locate them all. Some are injured, so they might be scattered. We'll be careful to keep our distance. If they seem hostile, it's important that we avoid a fight." He pressed harder on the lid. Every time he got one side down, the other popped up.

Twig held out her hand for it, and he turned it over before he could start a fight with a piece of plastic and pulverize what was left of the cookies.

"But we can't run, either."

"Right. We cannot show weakness." He fought the heat in his cheeks. He might not run from a charging enemy, but that little plastic box had just won his surrender. "We have a couple of options, depending on how they react. We can try to help and tame the injured—"

"That'll be tricky. The ones who are hurt are probably the ones who were more eager to attack us."

So much for hoping she wouldn't realize that. "True," he said. "And then we'd have to reintroduce them to the herd and hope the herd sees us as friends because they do. The other option is to try to establish Indy as the leader of the herd. He's familiar to all of them, but they accepted him and Wind Catcher as outsiders. They saw me and my father and our unicorns as a herd of our own. Could be, with Dagger gone, if they're looking for a leader and Indy steps into the role, they'll follow him. At least temporarily."

"They might challenge him."

Ben nodded. "I would be surprised if none of them did."

•••

A whistle sounded through the trees, similar to the one Ben used to call Emmie, his letter pigeon. On top of the tent, the emerald pigeon stirred and cooed.

"Stay there, Emmie," Ben said. Indy, then Wonder, nickered and pricked their ears in anticipation. "It's Merrill," Ben told Twig. He whistled back to Merrill.

Moments later, the branches parted and the old herder ducked in. "I wasn't sure I'd find you here, Ben-boy." Merrill raised his eyebrows at the tent. "I see our Twig-girl is here too."

"Just for a few days," Twig said. Merrill smiled, but he looked distracted and concerned. Twig glanced at Ben, at his crossed arms and his stiff posture. "What's the matter, Merrill?"

"It's the unicorn thief. He's struck again, and this time it's—"

"What unicorn thief?" Twig said. She sent Ben a sidelong glare. "Nobody told me about a unicorn thief."

"Someone's been stealing unicorns in Westland." Ben shifted restlessly. "Someone who's very, very good at it."

"But I thought all the unicorns in Westland belonged to the queen."

Merrill nodded solemnly. "Like Ben said, whoever it is, they're very good, and they're very bold. Stealing from the queen herself, and not just indirectly. Her own favorite mare was stolen right out of the castle stable just last week."

"Night Spark? Who would do that? Who would dare?"

"No one knows. And no one knows what he's doing with them."

"No one has any idea?" Twig said.

"Lots of people have ideas." Merrill rubbed the scar on his stubbly chin. "Ideas that don't bode well for the missing unicorns. Or for Terracornians." Merrill leaned back against a tree. "One rumor is that Eastland is behind the thefts. Though we're under a truce now, the wars have taken their toll. The unicorns' numbers are dwindling. Dangerously low. Likely they're stealing the best mounts for their own army and to breed new stock. But this particular theft suggests more."

"What do you mean, more?" Twig asked.

"War," Ben said. "Taking the queen's own unicorn—it's the ultimate insult."

Merrill nodded solemnly. "A blatant provocation."

Ben stared into the trees, deep in thought, eyes full of sadness.

Twig turned to Merrill. "I saw your note to Ben, about going to the queen. He won't tell me what it means. Does this have something to do with that? This unicorn thief? Starting a new war with Eastland?"

"Ahhh." Merrill looked surprised. "Yes, little one. I'm afraid it does."

"What!" Ben jerked to attention.

Merrill fixed Ben with a penetrating gaze. "What if Twig is right?"

He shook his head sharply. "It doesn't matter."

"It doesn't matter?" Twig said.

"This is my world now. This herd is my responsibility. Not Westland. There are no herders, no free unicorns allowed in Westland anymore, remember?"

"Your father—" Merrill began.

"My father left Westland, and for good reason. And this is what he left me—the unicorns of Lonehorn Island."

Chapter 6

IN HIS SHELTER, BEN awoke. The hollow was quiet, but the woods surrounding it were not. Merrill had gone back to Terracornus to look after Marble, the injured unicorn he was secretly caring for, and Ben and Twig were alone.

He pushed the sleeping bag back and grabbed his weapons, then pulled the boughs that formed the door of his shelter aside. A thick, misty morning seeped through the low-hanging branches of the hollow. So did sounds that made Ben's heart pound. Calls not nearly far enough away.

Unicorns.

But where was the low, warning answer from Indy? The neigh alerting his rider or young Wonder that a potential enemy was approaching? Ben glanced at the unicorns, still curled on their sides next to each other—they were not just in their usual lighter sleep, sitting with their legs bent under them, ready to rise in a blink, but in the truly deep sleep that only overtook them for a couple of hours each night. Usually in the deepest, darkest of the night. Not now, at sunrise!

It was unheard of for any unicorn. Ben grabbed Indy's tack and clambered out of his shelter.

Twig fell out of the tent, sword in hand. "You heard it too?"

Ben nodded. "They're headed this way."

Twig reached back inside the tent for her bow and quiver, then Wonder's tack.

"Why are they still sleeping?" Twig said. "We've got to wake them up."

Ben approached Indy carefully. He didn't want to startle him and get himself hurt. "Indy-boy. Let's get up now. Come on, we've got work to do."

Twig talked to Wonder, but neither animal stirred.

Ben rubbed Indy's neck. "Wake up, boy." The stallion didn't even open his eyes.

Outside the hollow, the unicorn calls grew louder. Ben rubbed Indy again, more briskly. Indy's eyelids lifted. His quicksilver eyes had a groggy, almost milky look.

"They must be sick." Twig rubbed Wonder's neck the same way and got no response.

Whatever the cause, their unicorns were dead asleep. And they could all be dead in moments if the herders didn't handle this right. The calls grew louder, dangerously close.

"Ben! What do we do? We can't just wait for them."

"We go out there. We defend the hollow." Ben slung his quiver over his shoulder and took up his bow.

"Without them?" Twig looked desperately at the sleeping unicorns.

"We have no choice."

Twig parted the branches, and Ben ducked out first, before she could. They stood there side by side in the morning mist, bows in hand, ready to aim and shoot. If only they could see their targets.

Ben's arm ached with tension. It seemed like ages before he spotted the ghostly white forms gliding through the fog.

The long, sharp horn of a majestic unicorn glittered in the mist. A pink scar marred its creamy coat—a wound inflicted by Ben. Two more horns appeared, bobbing in the dappled light and cutting through the fog. Three unicorns. They were outnumbered.

But instead of neighing a threat, the creatures called out softly, curiously. Ben had heard nothing but sounds of hunger, of vicious eagerness, of battle, and of pain from them for so long. "Don't shoot," he whispered to Twig. "Not yet."

"What do they want?"

"I'm not sure."

Should they try to drive them away from the hollow, or was it time to welcome them as friends? A surge of panic flowed through the already pounding pulse of action. Without Indy, he felt so vulnerable, empty-handed in spite of the weapons in his hands. If they charged and he and Twig didn't manage to shoot them first... *Father. Father, what should I do?*

Twig glanced at him nervously, expectantly. Her thin fingers curled, white with fear, around her bow.

"Breathe deep, Twig. Think calm. No fear. They'll sense it."

Twig nodded slowly. Three pale forms edged closer. Out of the corner of his eye, Ben watched Twig shut hers. Her lips moved a little. Talking to herself. Or to God. Praying. Her hands relaxed, and her eyes opened.

The unicorns snorted and sniffed. One of them pranced even closer, then circled back away—playfully?

They nickered at each other, and then they leaped away. A few yards into the trees, one of them paused and looked back.

"Hey there, friend." Ben gave the unicorn a reassuring nod. "It's good to see you again."

•••

Just moments after Twig and Ben ducked back into the hollow, Wonder and Indy opened their eyes and rose to their feet. They showed no signs of the strange, deep sleep. They sniffed the air curiously and nickered to each other, probably about the other unicorns that had come so close.

Twig was grateful they were all right and that she and Ben had had a peaceful encounter with the herd. Still, what had caused that odd, deep sleep? What if it happened again? What if one of the more aggressive wild unicorns sensed that they were vulnerable and tried to take them out?

Twig and Ben tacked up their unicorns and headed out of the hollow, in search of the herd. It seemed that at least a few of them were willing to consider the herders as something other than enemies—or prey. But how would they react to Indy and Wonder, whom Dagger had seen as such a threat?

Wonder sniffed and nickered to Indy. Indy sniffed too. He neighed softly in agreement.

"We're close," Ben said.

"To a unicorn?"

The ferns rustled a few yards away. Wonder lurched forward, but Twig pulled her back. "Whoa, girl," she said softly. "Not yet. Not like that."

Indy voiced his own low warning. Ben gave Twig a nod and motioned for her to back up while he and Indy went forward slowly, steadily. "Follow," he whispered, "just like this."

Wonder followed Indy, though her restraint was much more forced. An anguished cry came from the undergrowth. Ben and Indy stopped, and Twig reined Wonder in beside them. Wonder pinned her ears and peered into the flattened brush. A unicorn lay there with an ugly, enflamed gash on its side.

Ben looked a little like he was going to be sick. He sounded hoarse as he said, "That's Bounce. She always had a funny hop to her step."

An unsettling mixture of emotions burned in Twig's chest. "She has a name? Do all of them have names?"

"Of course. You cannot help naming a unicorn."

"But you never told me—I thought—"

Ben answered Twig in a soothing singsong tone that didn't match their conversation or Bounce's condition—a tone meant to keep Indy and Wonder at ease and to keep from pushing the already anxious wild unicorn over the edge. "Merrill and I thought it would be easier for you not to know."

"To see them as nameless wild things. As the enemy."

"They *were* the enemy when they attacked us."

Twig kept her mouth shut only because she knew she was starting to sound upset, and they were here to calm an injured unicorn. She thought of the gentle unicorn Merrill had lured away from the herd last winter with carrots and calming herbs. He'd called him Marble, and Twig had assumed Merrill had named him just then. Had Marble been *Marble* all along?

The unicorn had become tame, giving them all hope for the rest of the herd—until those very unicorns, Marble's own herd mates, had come and nearly killed Marble. In order to save him from Lonehorn Island's wayward herd, Merrill had to risk taking Marble back into Terracornus—where he would be considered an illegal unicorn and could be taken away, and Merrill punished severely. Merrill had been keeping Marble hidden at a safe house in Silverforest, Terracornus, ever since.

Twig jumped as the creature emitted a whine that verged on a growl. It seemed Bounce couldn't decide whether to scare them away or beg them for help.

"Hey there, Bounce." Ben drew a packet out of his pouch, careful not to make any sudden movements. "I brought you a little treat."

Ben tossed a ball of calming herbs mixed with chopped apples and wrapped in lettuce leaves. The unicorn startled, glared at them, then sniffed and nudged the packet. With one ear tuned to the humans, she lipped the lettuce.

"There now," Ben whispered. "We'll leave her to eat. In a little while, we'll come back and—"

Indy cried out in warning, and Wonder wheeled around. Bounce tried and failed to scramble to her feet. Another unicorn charged through the brush, horn tipped and ready to bore into Wonder.

Chapter 7

"Duck, Wonder!" Twig urged her unicorn to dodge
the attack rather than fight back. To Twig's relief,
Wonder complied. She landed right beside Bounce.

Indy stepped in and confronted their attacker, but instead of stabbing him, he locked horns. The wild unicorn
sidestepped and moved to slash, and again Indy blocked him
with his horn. On the other side of Twig, Bounce showed
Wonder her teeth.

Twig nudged Wonder back a step. "Easy, girl. She's just
scared. Let's show her we're friends."

Wonder relaxed. She nickered at the injured unicorn, a cautious greeting. The wild mare's ears tipped toward her with
interest. Instead of a snarl, she let out a blow.

Wonder neighed at Indy, *I think I found a new friend.* Indy,
horn still holding strong against the push of the other stallion's horn, neighed back. The wild stallion stepped back and
ducked his head, but this time it wasn't to charge. He bowed,
a gesture that said, *Okay, you win. You're stronger.*

Slowly, quietly, Ben dismounted and let the animals sniff each other. Twig did the same.

Ben held his hand out to the stallion. "Father called this one Ash," he whispered. "Because he looks like he stuck his nose in ashes."

Twig laughed softly. The stallion was pure white, except for his gray muzzle.

Maybe the herd really was going to be okay. "There's medicine that can help Bounce. They call it antibiotics."

"Do you have it? At the ranch?"

Twig's heart sank. "Mr. Murley brings the vet—the horse doctor—to the island, and she gives the sick pony a shot."

Ben's mouth formed a grim line. "We cannot do that."

"No, I guess not."

"But with food and water and some rest, she has a good chance. Wild unicorns get hurt and heal all the time, as long as they have everything else they need."

Twig nodded. She knelt in the ferns a couple feet away from Bounce. The unicorn eyed her warily. Twig whispered a prayer that she would be okay.

Beside her, Ben lowered himself to one knee. "Amen," he whispered.

They sat there for a moment, and they watched, and they hoped.

Wonder nibbled Twig's ear. It tickled, and Twig laughed.

Behind them, Indy and Ash nickered their own horsey laughs. Ash stepped around the two riders, keeping a careful eye on them. He sniffed at Bounce, then went for the bundle of food and herbs. Twig moved to leap up, to stop him from taking it from Bounce, but Ben held her back.

Twig watched as Ash nudged the packet right under Bounce's nose, urging her to eat.

"Well." Ben took Twig's sleeve as he rose. "Looks like she's taken care of for now."

•••

A couple of days later, before Ben took Twig and Wonder back to the ranch, they headed to the spot where they'd left Bounce. They carried bags of feed—enough for two unicorns. Ash had gone off on his own when they'd first returned to feed and check on the injured Bounce, but not far. He'd come to watch them from a distance. This morning, he was there by Bounce's side.

They delivered the food without incident, then a bucket of water from a little creek nearby. The herders and their unicorns kept their distance, except to place the bucket and the feed within reach. Twig was pleased to see Bounce stand to drink from the bucket.

"It's strange to see them like this."

"This is how they were," Ben said wistfully, "before. Ash isn't as fierce as some. It might not be so easy with the others. But it's a start. A nice start."

"This is the first day I've really felt like a herder." Twig smiled sheepishly.

Ben met her eyes with a serious gaze. "May it be the first of many."

Stay, Twig. You have to find a way to stay. She heard the unspoken words. She heard them, but she had no answer. No answer but good-bye.

"She's looking better," she whispered. At least she'd gotten to see that before she had to go.

"Ready?" Ben said.

Twig nodded. "I miss the Murleys and Rain Cloud and the girls…"

"And the food." Ben grinned.

"You should come in and stay for dinner before you go."

"No…I wouldn't want anyone to change their minds."

CHAPTER 8

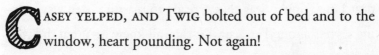

ASEY YELPED, AND TWIG bolted out of bed and to the window, heart pounding. Not again!

Bam!

The last time Twig had wakened to banging in the night, it had been Dagger and the wild herd, on the verge of breaking through the stable doors to get at Wonder. But this was more of a tapping, and it was closer. Outside the window, night hung heavy over the ranch, the sky lightened only by the mist. Anyone could be out there. Anything.

Bam, bam.

"It's a knock," Twig realized with relief. Just someone knocking.

"Ben!" both the girls said at once.

They bounded to the door, Casey clutching her battered old doll to her chest. Twig threw the bedroom door open. All along the hallway, bedroom doors opened and girls called out anxiously.

Mr. Murley was already at the front door, hair standing on end, shotgun in hand. Mrs. Murley gathered the other girls in the entryway and tried to hold them back, just in case. Casey's arms shook as she squished the cloth body of her doll. Its heavily lashed eyelids rattled open and shut.

"What if it's not Ben? What if someone else came from Terracornus?" Casey said.

Twig waited for someone to say that was impossible, but no one did—not skeptical Regina, not practical Taylor, not upbeat Janessa, who was always ready to reassure. Ben was keeping secrets about Terracornus; they all knew it. What did they really know about Terracornus or its people? Would someone come after Ben? Could they?

Twig recalled the first time Ben had led her through the terrifyingly thick ring of mist in the center of the island, then through another circle, this one formed by hemlock trees whose branches swept to the forest floor. They guarded the ancient passage tree, a red cedar whose trunk held a hidden door that led to Terracornus. Ben wore a key to that door around his neck, and so did Merrill. "I'm not the only one with a key," Ben had told her. Who else had a key besides him and Merrill?

Twig ducked around the others so she could slide the locks open, while Mr. Murley kept the shotgun trained on the door. She opened it a crack.

Ben stood there, gasping. He flung the door against the wall before Twig had a chance to let him in. "It's Indy. He's gone. He's just—gone!"

"Is he dead?" Casey said.

"No!" Ben said too firmly. "He's disappeared. He won't answer when I call. I cannot find him anywhere."

Mr. Murley said, "Come inside, Ben, and we'll figure this out."

Ben grabbed Twig's arm. "You have to come. You have to help me."

"Definitely." Twig reached for her all-weather shell.

"Wonder will know where Indy went. She's his daughter and part of his herd. She'll follow his scent and find him," Ben said.

"Whoa." Mrs. Murley tucked her mussed-up brown hair behind her ear. Her face was creased with sleep and concern. "Ben, why don't you come in first and tell us everything?"

Twig pulled her jacket the rest of the way on and reached for her boots. "We don't have time. We have to find Indy!"

But Mrs. Murley pulled Ben in.

Twig carried her boots as she followed everyone to the living room.

Ben paced in front of the couch, cape and boots still on, ready to jump into action in an instant.

"Ben," Mr. Murley said, "is Merrill here on the island?"

"No, he's not here. I was in the hollow, sound asleep. I thought I heard Indy neigh. I got up and looked outside, and he wasn't there. He always stays there under his favorite tree at night. Guarding me. Protecting me. He never leaves."

Twig leaned on the arm of the couch beside him. "Something's wrong." A hardness settled in her gut. "We're wasting time here. Let's go get Wonder and find him."

"Hold on," Mr. Murley said. "It's the middle of the night."

"But I'm a herder!" Twig said. "A unicorn is in danger. I have to go."

Mrs. Murley slipped an arm around Twig. "And we took on the responsibility of protecting you. Of course you're worried about Indy. It *is* strange. But the herd has been doing so well. Do you really think they're a danger to Indy?"

They all stilled, listened. The night was perfectly calm. Not a howl or a cry. Just the misty breeze ruffling the cedars.

"No," Ben conceded.

"It's quiet out there," Mandy pointed out. "Not like before, when they were all crazy."

Janessa gave Mandy a sharp poke.

Mrs. Murley said, "You can sleep here tonight, Ben, and we'll all go in the morning."

It was all Twig could do to hold back her protest. Ben looked like he was about to explode.

"I'll get the blankets." Janessa bounced off to the linen closet.

Mr. Murley ran a hand over his rumpled hair. "Indy's made for the woods. He knows how to handle himself on this island."

"And he knows not to leave his post!" Ben said. "He wouldn't just wander away."

"Maybe he heard or smelled something unusual and went to investigate," Taylor said. "Animals can be curious just like we are."

Ben shook his head, too angry now to speak. But Twig had a plan. If only she could talk to Ben alone.

Janessa plopped an armful of blankets onto the couch. Ben just stood there, arms crossed, brooding. The sleeves of the barn jacket Mrs. Murley had given him were smeared with sap, and bits of lichen stuck to it. Clearly he knew nothing about dealing with parents. Twig tried to catch his eye to send him a signal to cooperate, but his gaze was fixed on the floor-to-ceiling windows, as though looking hard enough would make Indy appear, gleaming silver-white, through the darkness.

CHAPTER 9

IT SEEMED LIKE FOREVER that Twig lay in bed, listening and waiting, watching the glowing red numbers on her bedside clock. How long should she wait? An hour? Two? After forty-five minutes, she couldn't take it anymore. Indy was missing. What if he was sick or hurt and confused? What was so dangerous about going into the woods at night now that Dagger was gone?

Twig's heart squeezed with the answer. *It is dangerous.* Dagger might not be out there anymore, but something was. Something that had everything to do with Indy going missing.

Twig slipped out of bed.

"I knew it!" Casey said it in a whisper, but Twig still jumped. She'd thought Casey was asleep. Casey had gotten good at faking it. She hopped up, short brown hair bobbing. "You have to take me with you this time, please, Twig."

"Ben would never let me do that, not without Indy."

There was a pronounced plop on the bed and a muffled utterance of disappointment, the kind that might be followed by tears. She didn't have time to console Casey. She had to find Indy. She got dressed, slipped on her mini-backpack, and tiptoed to the door.

"I'm sorry," she whispered over her shoulder. Then she eased the door open and shut it softly behind her.

Twig stopped. She heard voices. Whispers, and not from the girls. Mr. and Mrs. Murley were still awake. Should she go back?

"Do you really think someone could've come here?" Mrs. Murley said. "From Terracornus?"

"I don't know. They haven't before…but I can't stop thinking about those boot prints I saw in the woods earlier. Too big to be Ben's. I thought they were Merrill's, but Ben just said he's back in Terracornus."

Mrs. Murley said something Twig couldn't make out.

Mr. Murley changed his tone. "I'm sure Indy's out there now, at Ben's camp, wondering where he is. But we can't take that chance."

"Those girls are too brave for their own good. Ben's worse."

Mr. Murley laughed softly. "Not worse than Twig. Not anymore."

Twig couldn't help sticking her chin up at that. She crept into the living room. The fog was thick, and little moonlight shone through the wall of windows on the far side of the room. Twig inched closer to a blanketed lump on one end of the huge sectional couch. She put her hand out to nudge Ben awake and then she heard it—a light thump.

It came from somewhere inside the house. Someone else was up. Twig ducked behind the couch and waited for Mr. or Mrs. Murley to call out. Maybe they'd heard her and gotten up to investigate. But she hadn't heard a door open, hadn't heard a sound in the hall.

Another whisper of movement. This time she was sure it came from the entryway. Someone was there, and they were making an effort not to be heard.

Casey?

Twig sneaked out from behind the couch and flattened herself against the wall. She peeked around the corner, then pulled back quickly, heart pounding. A shadowy figure loomed over the threshold, too tall, too broad shouldered to be any of the girls.

Twig darted back to the couch, to Ben. "Ben!" she whispered urgently. "Wake up!" She reached Ben's sleeping form and gave it a good shake.

"Yes?"

The voice came from behind her. Twig jerked around. She stopped her scream just in time. Ben stood over her, cape and boots on, finger held to his lips.

Twig sank onto the pile of blankets—empty blankets that ought to have been wrapped around a sleeping Ben.

"What," Ben whispered sharply, "are you doing? Getting a late-night snack?"

Twig jumped to her feet. Hands on her hips, she glared at Ben. "What are *you* doing? Were you going to take Wonder without me?"

Ben crossed his arms. "I wouldn't take another rider's unicorn. Not even to save my own!" The words were more than sharp this time; they came out like grit.

Twig looked at her feet. She didn't want him to see what she'd just realized written all over her face. She might be tempted to take another rider's unicorn if she were in Ben's position. It seemed such an obvious solution.

"I wasn't going to take Wonder," Ben said, sounding more like himself. "I'm going to go look for Indy again."

"By yourself?"

"I cannot just sit here. I certainly cannot sleep."

"Well, you can't just walk out the front door either. They'll hear you for sure."

"How did you get out all those times when you came to practice at night?" Ben asked.

"Through my window. Come on." She pointed at Ben's boots. "Take those off. They'll hear you in the hall."

She tiptoed to the entryway to pick up her boots and her all-weather shell. Ben followed. He sat down on the entryway floor and pulled off his boots. "What are we doing?"

"Getting Wonder, of course. And then going to find Indy."

He looked her up and down. "You planned this." She was fully dressed, in jeans and not in the sweats she typically wore to bed.

"I couldn't say anything in front of everyone else. Did you really think I'd just go to sleep? I know I'm not your dad, but we're partners now, aren't we? And you know I love Indy. How could you try to go out there without me?"

Ben mumbled something about reading her mind, then grabbed his boots and followed her silently back to her room. The whispers from the Murleys' room could no longer be heard.

Casey sat up and stared at Twig and Ben, mouth clenched shut, hot pink comforter clutched tight in her hands. Ben gave her a polite, tentative wave.

Casey's lips trembled. "I'm going to be in trouble for not stopping you. *Big* trouble."

Twig put her boots on and gestured for Ben to do the same. "I'm sorry, Casey. We'll make it up to you."

Casey yanked her covers over her head and curled into a little ball. Ben gave Twig a perplexed look. She shrugged and slid the window open. The misty chill reached into the bedroom, drawing them into its night-cold grasp. The huddle of pink covers shuddered. Twig gestured for Ben to go out first.

Twig dropped to the ground and slid the window shut, sealing Casey and the rest of the house off from the island chill.

It wasn't difficult taking Wonder without a fuss from her or the ponies. The stable's inhabitants were used to Twig creeping inside in the deep of night and leading Wonder into the woods to train. Not wanting the ponies to think something out of the ordinary was going on, Ben left Twig to get Wonder alone. He went ahead, on foot, to the hollow.

As Twig leaped the fence with Wonder and bounded into the trees, her stomach tightened. Ben was out here alone. She should've had him wait at the fence and walked Wonder with him. What if whoever had taken Indy was waiting for him?

"Ben?" Twig called as soon as she was near enough to the hollow.

"I'm here!"

She heard his breath and the flap of his cape before he appeared, running through the mist. Twig dismounted. "What do we do now?"

"We wait for Wonder. She'll find Indy's scent."

Twig reached for the flashlight in the pocket of her shell, then pulled her hand back out without it. They couldn't risk anyone seeing it, even as they ventured deeper into the woods. The Murleys might come looking—and someone else could be watching.

At first Wonder just neighed into the blanket of fog. Twig watched the woods anxiously. She hoped the wrong unicorns wouldn't respond. Even if some of the wild ones came, meaning no harm, things could so easily go wrong between them and young, inexperienced Wonder.

Wonder sniffed the boughs that sheltered the hollow, then leaped away. Twig scrambled after her in the dark. She caught her lead as she stopped to sniff again. Twig wound Wonder's lead securely around her wrist just in time. Wonder lurched onward.

"Hold on, Wonder. Slow, girl."

Wonder neighed her reluctance, but, not quite willing to drag her rider through the undergrowth, she obeyed.

"Twig!" Ben stumbled into her back as Wonder jerked to a stop. He grabbed the back of her jacket to catch himself.

Twig reached backward and groped for his hand. He took her hand and held on fast.

"She's found his scent." Ben's voice was tight with hope, with impatience and anticipation.

"She must've. She wants to go this way really bad."

Wonder plunged on through the damp ferns and the branches coated with moss and draped with lichen. Twig hung on to her lead for dear life, and Ben slipped and slid after them.

"Twig! Tell her to stop."

"What? Why? Are you okay?"

"I'm fine, just"—he lowered his voice—"did you hear something?"

"Whoa, Wonder. Just a minute now."

Wonder pranced in place.

"Shh!" Ben hissed.

"I can't make her be quiet. She wants to go."

"I think I just heard it again."

"If there were other unicorns around us, Wonder would know. Her horn would extend."

"Not other unicorns. Something else."

"What else?"

Before Ben could answer, Wonder bounced forcefully. Twig yelped and ran after her with Ben in tow. The mist thickened, and the belt of fear tightened around Twig's gut. "She's taking us to the center of the island."

"To the hemlock circle," Ben panted between breaths. "The passage."

"Whoa, Wonder." Twig glanced back at Ben. "If Indy's in Terracornus—"

Wonder pranced in a tight circle. Twig turned to face Ben.

Just as he opened his mouth to speak, something crashed in the undergrowth nearby. There was a faint moan, a gasp.

"Who's there?" Ben's hand left Twig's and grasped his sword. But the only sound was the smooth slide of steel as he drew his weapon.

Wonder nickered at the wall of thicker fog. She nipped at it, then bounced back again. Wonder called for Indy, as though afraid to enter but knowing she must do it in order to find him. Wonder paid no attention to the woods behind them. To the sounds.

"Maybe it was just a raccoon," Twig whispered.

"Could be," Ben said. "Let's go. Let her go on."

The branches of the hemlock circle swept down to the forest floor, another circle within the ring of mist, keeping the passage hidden. Wonder squealed in distaste at the branches, and no doubt at taking another step closer to Terracornus. Like all unicorns, she instinctively knew she was close to leaving her world, and she dreaded it. But she also longed for Indy. Ben held the boughs back for Wonder as best he could, and Twig soothed her as she made her way through.

"Your flashlight," Ben said.

Twig fumbled in her pocket, found it, and flipped it on.

"Here, on the ground."

Twig shone the light on the ground. Ben knelt next to a series of hoofprints.

"He came through here for sure." Twig moved her flashlight a few inches over.

Ben locked eyes with her. "So did someone else."

CHAPTER 10

WITH HIS SWORD, BEN pointed to the human boot prints ground into the cedar-red dirt. He shivered and pulled his cloak tighter around him, over the coat Mrs. Murley had given him.

"They're too small for Merrill, and they follow right alongside the unicorn," Ben said.

"Someone's taken him to Terracornus," Twig said. "Who? How?"

Wonder neighed her impatience.

"We're going, Wonder," Ben assured her. "We're going to find out."

But Twig held Wonder back. "I can't just disappear in there, Ben. What about the Murleys?"

"Twig!"

Ben whirled around at the cry. It was muffled by the hemlock branches, but soon a crashing followed, and a small body hurtled through and skidded onto the patch of cleared earth around the passage tree.

"You have to go!" Casey cried, still prone on the ground.

"Casey!"

Through the branches, a hand appeared, groping for Casey's. Taylor. Janessa trailed behind her, clutching her hand. Then Regina and Mandy. A chain of girls tumbled into the secret heart of the island, wincing at their scrapes and crawling through the shadows, trying to find their feet.

"All of you?" Twig said.

Oh no. Not all of them. Ben groaned. He turned to Twig. "They cannot be here. I've broken the herders' trust."

"Maybe," Casey said a little guiltily, a little hopefully, "we could all be herders too."

"No!" Twig said. "No way. How could you do this? I trusted you."

"Don't yell at her!" Regina cried. "We wanted to see! It isn't fair, hearing all the stories and not even getting to see."

"There isn't really another world, is there?"

That was Mandy, the blond one who was constantly frowning at Ben. Twig said she was always like that, but he wasn't so sure.

Mandy narrowed her eyes at him. "That's why you don't want us here."

You have no idea what I would give for you not to be here right now. He'd rather face the famous rider and tournament champion Reynald the Boy King than the scrutiny of these girls. He wanted to take Indy and just ride. Ride away from all of these people who wanted something from him. Even the herd. He imagined Indy gallop-gliding, away from everything, out of the trees and over the rocks along the shore, right off the island, right on top of the water. There was a wider world out there. There must be somewhere for a unicorn to go. Somewhere to just be. Twig and Wonder could come, but—

It didn't matter. Indy was missing. There was no escaping that.

"No one is supposed to be here." He ground out the words. *This place is mine and my father's.* It was a secret. Ben had been so alone without him and then so glad to have Twig. But this was too much. He didn't have Indy, and it was too much.

"We don't have time for this," Twig said. "I don't know how you found us, but you're all going to have to find your way back."

"But we followed you," Taylor said. "And it's dark."

"And this mist is creepy!" Regina hugged herself against its chill.

"It's definitely *not* normal," Mandy agreed.

"Twig." Ben gestured for her to shine her flashlight on the bark of the ancient red cedar, the passage tree, so he could find the hidden keyhole quicker.

Ben pulled the key out from under his shirt, where he kept

it on a chain. He reached out to unlock the door, and he stared at the tree, stunned. He dropped the key.

"Casey, keep back. You're blocking the light!" Twig was oblivious to what Ben had seen.

The key swung against his chest, safe on its chain, but his hand trembled as he reached for a white square of paper pinned to the passage tree. He pulled it off and held it in Twig's flashlight beam.

"What's that?" The girls shushed each other and crowded around him.

He needed more light. He grabbed Mandy's flashlight and illuminated the message.

Taylor peered over his shoulder and read it aloud. "'The fate of one is the fate of them all. Now you know what it is like for those of us who still care about *all* unicorns. If you want to see your unicorn again, keep your oath and go to the queen.'"

"Is it a note from Merrill?" Janessa said.

"It's not from Merrill," Twig said, taking a peek. "That's not his handwriting."

"And it's signed 'The Unicorn Thief'!" Taylor said.

"Who's that? What does it mean?" Casey said.

Twig just shook her head. Her eyes asked Ben the same question.

"I never made an oath to go to the queen!" Ben pulled

himself together. "Forget the note. What matters is that Indy's in there for sure. He's gone through the passage."

Taylor put her hand to the cedar trunk. "This tree is the passage?"

Twig touched Ben's arm. "We'll find him."

But Mandy said, "It's a trap."

"Don't go, Twig," Taylor added.

And Janessa said, "Mandy's right this time."

"It's up to Twig. She's Wonder's rider. Her life and Wonder's will be at risk." Ben fought to keep his voice steady, his heart from bursting, his terror from bringing him to his knees. He had no right to ask Twig for this.

Wonder sniffed and pawed away at the dirt. She whinnied her fear and yearning. That was her father in there.

"We are *not* going to leave Indy in Terracornus all by himself," Twig said. "Besides, there's no deciding for me to do. If we don't let Wonder through the passage tree, she'll dig it up by the roots." Twig turned to Ben. "She hates coming here, but she didn't fight it, the whole way. She wants to go in. She knows something. She can smell it."

"Twig—" Ben began to protest.

"Didn't you and Merrill tell me to trust my unicorn?"

"Wait," Regina said, "why would anyone try to trap Ben? They already have Indy."

"To get Wonder too," Casey said.

"But how would anyone over there know about Wonder? Unless—" Mandy gasped and clamped a hand over mouth.

"What?" Twig said.

A new chill shuddered through Ben. "Merrill." His old friend's name barely came out. His mouth felt so dry.

Mandy nodded. "Your herder friend's been hiding from the cops over there with that unicorn he's not supposed to have."

"Cops?" Another Earth Land word Ben didn't know.

"The authorities," Taylor explained.

"What if they caught him and…" Twig couldn't finish.

But Regina said, "Tortured him or something. Do they do stuff like that there?"

Ben felt strangely numb. This couldn't be happening. What if he lost Merrill too?

"We'll make sure Merrill's okay before we go in. But," Twig warned the girls, "even if he isn't okay, that doesn't mean we're not going. Ben, call Emmie. Casey, you go back with the others and get Rain Cloud. Ben will need a ride."

Of course. They wouldn't get far in Terracornus on foot. Wonder was only a year old and not strong enough to carry both of them.

"What about Feather?" Casey suggested.

Twig shook her head. "We can't take Mrs. Murley's horse."

"That would be like stealing," Janessa agreed.

"You would know," Regina said, making a jab at Janessa's past.

Ben didn't know why all the other girls were living with the Murleys, but for some reason Janessa had confessed her thievery to him. She'd been proud to add that she hadn't taken "a darn thing" in over a year.

The girls kept bickering. "That's enough!" Ben's numbness blew off in a blast of anger. "Stop picking at each other. You're family!"

The girls exchanged skeptical glances.

"You're all you have anyway. More than I have!"

Twig's flashlight glow glinted off her eyes, strikingly blue, shining with tears. "You have us, Ben," she whispered. "You have us too."

"We're sorry," Janessa said. They all nodded and murmured their agreement. Mist-damp heads bowed.

Ben ducked his head and rubbed quickly at his eyes. *Crying.* For pity's sake, standing here crying in front of all these silly girls.

Twig reached for Ben's arm. "Indy—he's not all you have now, Ben. But he *is* a lot. We're going to get him back."

Yes, he is *all I have!* Ben wanted to shout. *He's all I want. He's never let me down.*

But what if Indy *had* let him down? He'd gone quietly back to Terracornus. He'd left Ben sleeping in the hollow. He'd gone with someone else, without a cry of protest, without a whinny of good-bye.

CHAPTER 11

WONDER HESITATED AT THE open door to the passage, then sniffed again and plunged through the tunnel of the hollowed-out tree so fast that Twig had to release the reins in order to get out of her way.

Rain Cloud plodded after Wonder. He shook his head in disapproval at the dark, narrow space. It had taken Ben and Twig and all the other girls—and ultimately Wonder's pleas for the old pony to follow her—to get Rain Cloud through the low-hanging hemlock boughs that encircled the passage tree. Ben wrapped Rain Cloud's reins around his wrist. He returned the pony's gaze of near terror with one as close to confidence as he could muster.

The girls stood there five in a row, hand in hand, faces lit by the faint beam of Mandy's flashlight. They'd made it back to the passage with Rain Cloud, without any run-ins with the herd. Ben gave them a wave good-bye and shut the passage door, then locked it.

After about an hour, Emmie had found Merrill and returned

with a hastily written reply; he was going to meet them at an old herders' outpost not far from the passage. He urged them to stay off the road, to stay hidden as much as possible.

Ben led Rain Cloud through the passage, into Terracornus. The misty air surrounding the Terracornus side of the passage filled Ben's lungs—a different air than that of the island. Heavier, thick with the fragrance of new silverfire leaves. It would grow even more pungent with the warmth of day.

He'd loved that smell when he was younger. The smell of being with Father, with his herdsmen in Silverforest. Working hard, yet free. He used to long for it every day on the island. Now the aroma of peace had become the scent of fear. The leaves whispered of freedom gone. When the wind blew, the forest groaned for what it wanted to be again. Morning dew dripped from the leaves—tears for the distant cries of unicorns, carried by the wind from the battlefields and training grounds beyond the forest where they toiled and bled. Would the trail of Indy's scent lead them there?

• • •

Wonder carried Twig through Silverforest, head bent in determination. Every now and then, she paused to sniff at the ground or the brush, and Rain Cloud stopped to pant and bellow his protest at being pushed so hard.

Purple blossoms covered some of the smaller trees. Fallen flowers formed patches of mauve carpet, softening the forest floor. New leaves were unfolding overhead, bright, pale green in the glow of the sunshine. It was hard for Twig to imagine Terracornus being a place unicorns would want to escape. Hard to believe it was a dangerous, warlike place.

Wonder circled back and nipped at Rain Cloud to try to get him to pick up the pace. Emmie swooped overhead, cooing down at them as though she too were urging Rain Cloud to hurry.

Rain Cloud showed Wonder his teeth and dug in his heels, refusing to be pushed.

"Twig, can you not get her to stop doing that? She's only making things worse."

"I'm trying."

"They're both impossible!" Ben snapped.

Rain Cloud's eyes were wide with fear. Twig could tell he wanted nothing but to run, to flee back home. He neighed for Wonder to go with him, but she whinnied her refusal.

Emmie settled on Ben's shoulder, her bright green plumage contrasting with the white feathers in his quiver. She pecked sympathetically at his cheek, but he had no smile for his faithful bird. Twig had never seen Ben so on edge like this.

They turned a corner, and a little grassy clearing came into view. The rocky, weedy road faded into the clearing. A low building squatted in the middle of the yard, a tiny square of rough-hewn stones nearly overtaken by the weeds that had risen up around it and taken root on its roof. A pair of dangling, rusty hinges hinted that it had once had an actual door that shut.

Stone posts, covered in a patchwork of moss and fitted with iron rings, poked out of the grass. Tethered to one of these was a donkey, chewing on the grass with a look of bored distaste. Wonder called out to the donkey, anxious, pleading. The donkey seemed to give a halfhearted little snort of recognition.

"Franklin knows Indy," Ben said. "He smells him on Wonder."

Twig slid down and stretched her back while Ben dismounted.

Wonder hopped over to Franklin, the donkey. She danced around the animal in tighter and tighter circles. *I need to find my dad. Where's my dad? You know him, don't you?*

Rain Cloud pretended not to notice the donkey or Wonder's behavior until the unicorn got just one circle too close to Franklin. The donkey's hind legs shot out. Wonder bounced back, avoiding the kick. Rain Cloud darted between them and nipped a warning at Franklin.

Twig caught Wonder's reins, and Ben took hold of Rain Cloud.

"Hey now," Ben said. "Both of you be nice to Franklin. Merrill needs him. He'd rather have his old Lion Heart, but there's no helping that, is there?"

Lion Heart had been Merrill's last unicorn, taken for the queen's army when the herders were disbanded. He'd died in a battle training accident. Merrill didn't like to talk about it.

Twig guided Wonder farther away from Franklin. "Maybe Marble will be well enough for Merrill to ride soon."

"Could be." Ben held his hand out to Rain Cloud. "You're a good boy. It's not easy trying to keep up with our Wonder, is it? I thank you for the ride."

Rain Cloud grunted his acceptance and let Ben lead him away. He shot one last toothy warning at Franklin.

"Merrill!" Ben called.

There was a shuffle-thump inside the shelter, and Merrill appeared in the doorway. He filled a stone trough next to Franklin with fresh water, then kept the donkey out of the way so the unicorn and the pony could drink.

"Best tether Wonder behind the shelter, Twig. Just to be safe," Merrill advised.

Twig nodded to Ben. "Rain Cloud too. He'll help keep her quiet."

"We cannot stay long," Ben said. "We cannot afford to lose Indy's trail."

"Just a short rest," Merrill assured him. "And a moment for me to think if there's a thing I can do to help. Then I'll give you what you need and send you on your way."

Once they had the animals settled—as settled as Wonder

could get—Merrill said, "Well, come inside, the two of you, where it's warm. The fire's going fine."

Flames glowed in the shadowy interior of the shelter, inviting even in its barrenness. Merrill had spread his familiar thick woolen blanket near the hearth on the dirt floor. They all sat down, and a heavy, quiet sadness filled their little circle.

Emmie fluttered into the doorway. She hopped tentatively to Ben and rubbed her head against his arm. He took a pinch of seeds from his pocket, and Emmie jumped onto his lap.

"Well," Merrill said, "better tell me what happened, Ben-boy, so we can find your Indy."

Ben blinked. Twig knew that look. If he opened his mouth, he was going to cry. Dependable, unshakable, brave Ben. So Twig told Merrill everything she knew.

"And then there was this." She drew the note out of her pocket and passed it to Merrill. "It was pinned to the passage tree."

Merrill scanned the note. He drew in a sharp breath. "The unicorn thief has access to the passage. And he wants something from you, Ben."

CHAPTER 12

BEN ROSE AND WENT to the fire. He picked up the poker stick and jabbed at the logs.

"But why would someone who wants to start a war between Eastland and Westland want Indy? How would someone from Eastland even know about Indy?" Ben shook his head. Emmie flapped off his lap, back to the doorway. "I'm not going to go to the queen just because this thief told me to. I won't be threatened like this! How do I even know I'll get Indy back? If someone will steal, he'll lie too."

Twig cringed inside. She'd stolen things, back when she'd lived with Mom. Stolen things for her mom. *But I'm different now*, she told herself. *A new Twig.* A Twig who could take back what was stolen this time. "Maybe the queen would be grateful that we could help find her unicorn." Maybe she could even be persuaded to change her ways. Twig got up so she could look Ben in the eye. "If she'd offer us protection—"

"The queen protects no one! She has no idea what she's

done, what she's doing to all of us!" Ben's hand clenched around the stick. He spun around and tossed it at the far wall.

Merrill was on his feet with a quick jerk. "Then I suppose you'll have to let her know—about a number of things."

Ben stiffened, then deflated. Merrill's words had not only burst the balloon of anger, but had also sucked all the heat and life out of him.

Twig spoke up. "I don't know what's going on here. But I do know that this thief—and who knows who else—has been going through the passage. Strangers, on our island. Our home, Ben. Sneaking around in the dark." The passage was supposed to be locked. And then she remembered—"Only the queen can change the locks! You told me that once. She could change the locks, couldn't she? We wouldn't have to worry about who has a key now or how they got it. As long as she only gave us one. Everything could be how it was. We could go back and work with the herd—"

"Nothing can ever be how it was!" Ben's eyes shone with unshed tears. "I'm sorry," he said gruffly. "I don't know…this whole thing is…"

"It isn't just Indy you miss. You miss him still…your dad." And he was afraid of losing Indy forever, just like he'd lost Darian. "Couldn't you *try* talking to the queen?" Twig said gently.

"She's the last person I'd ask for help."

Ben turned away with a snap of his cape. The flames flickered at his back, and the fire was back in his eyes.

Twig was about to snap back in her frustration. But she knew what it was to not want to ask for things, didn't she?

Outside, Wonder cried out, her whinny strained with thinning patience, tinged with the threat of total rebellion. Rain Cloud nickered a reprimand, a reassurance, but his anxiousness was unmistakable too. Franklin's bray from the other side of the shelter topped off the animals' complaints.

"It's time we get going," Ben said coolly. "Do you have what we need?"

"Of course." Merrill nodded toward the corner of the shelter, at what appeared to be a pile of folded clothes.

Twig followed Ben to the corner, where Merrill handed her a black tunic trimmed in red and yellow.

Ben took off his cape and slipped an identical garment over his shirt. "We're messengers for the queen's army."

Twig put her tunic on over her shell and mini-backpack, then turned to Merrill. "Maybe you should come with us."

"I have to get back home to Marble. I'm too well-known in certain circles besides. Too distinctive." He patted his artificial leg.

"Oh." Twig glanced sideways at Ben. She didn't know how she was going to handle a stubborn pony, a wild-hearted unicorn, and this boy—just as stubborn and wild with grief and determination. Just as strange to her, as secretive as this world, hidden from the Earth Land by its circle of mist.

Merrill picked up a harness and bridle, adorned with black fabric and trimmed in red and yellow, just like Twig's tunic. "Time to outfit Wonder and Rain Cloud."

"How did you get this stuff?"

Merrill shrugged. "I've been working on it ever since I found out about you and your Wonder. Since I heard of Darian's fate. I wanted to be prepared in case the two of you had to spend some time in Terracornus. Trouble is, I hadn't planned on outfitting a pony. I'm afraid a grown unicorn's trappings will make an awkward fit for little Rain Cloud."

"We'll make it do," Ben said.

"But still, Rain Cloud *is* a pony. I mean, are there even ponies here in Terracornus?"

"There are horses, sure. They do the hauling and the plowing."

"The grunt work," Ben put in.

"But not ponies," Twig said.

"Well..."

Ben said, "It's a good enough reason for him to be made a messenger. A stunted horse. Too small for heavier work."

"Stunted!" They'd probably think Twig was stunted too, small and skinny as she was. People didn't call her *Twig* for nothing.

Ben said, "You'll have to think like a Terracornian from time to time in order to survive among them."

Twig spun on her heel and headed for the open doorway. "If that's how Terracornians think, then I'm glad I'm not one of them."

A hand rested on Twig's back. "You could never be one," Ben said. "Your heart's too big."

"They can change, you know," Merrill said. "Terracornus wasn't always this way. We must never forget that."

Twig shifted uncomfortably in the tunic. "If this world can turn one way, it can turn back the other," she said hopefully.

But Ben didn't look so sure.

Behind the shelter, they draped Rain Cloud and Wonder with the trappings.

Merrill gave the animals a confident nod. "We're ready for the last bit, looks like." He held a white disc in the palm of his hand. Fine leather straps dangled from it, over his arm. "Twig, we're going to need your help with this."

Twig's fingers tightened in Wonder's mane. "What is it?"

"A horn cap, to keep Wonder's horn down."

Twig's stomach knotted up. "Why would we want to do that?"

"Because," Ben said quietly, "the only reason a fine yearling unicorn like Wonder would be a messenger, the only reason she wouldn't be training for battle instead, is if there was a flaw with her horn."

"Misshapen, blunted, broken, missing..." Merrill said.

"So when she's wearing this and she's around other uni-corns, her horn won't extend?"

"It cannot," Merrill explained. "The pressure keeps it down."

"She isn't going to like this, is she?"

"No, Twig." Merrill put a hand on her shoulder. "I'll put it on her. Let her blame me."

"Merrill..."

"He's right. You'll hate it, and she'll feel it while you're strapping it on."

Thank God Wonder's horn was already retracted. Merrill was so steady, Wonder only squirmed the slightest bit. He buckled the straps over her ears and under her chin. Twig adjusted her bridle to cover the horn cap's straps, then arranged Wonder's silky forelock over the disk.

Merrill said, "There's some food packed up for the two of you, for your journey. Come and help me get it, Twig."

"Sure."

Inside the shelter, Twig said, "Thank you, Merrill, for everything."

"Of course." Merrill shook her hand, then pulled her into a hug. "You take care, Twig."

Twig glanced out the door. Ben was leading Rain Cloud around the front already. Twig moved to go, but Merrill held her hand tight. He whispered, "A true friend is a rare thing, for anybody. A friend of any sort is rare enough for that boy. I know you're true, Twig. And I know you'll convince him to go to the queen." Merrill leaned closer. "He thinks Darian wouldn't want him to go to her, and could be he's right. But even so, going to her is what's right."

Twig didn't know what to say. She hadn't really had friends either before she came to the Murleys. The girls were her friends now, truly; she was sure of that. So was Ben. But could she really influence someone like him? "I'll try," she said.

Merrill clapped her on the back. He gave her a confident smile. "You've got the heart of a herder. A herder from the old days. Days when we'd never give up on a single unicorn, let alone their whole kind. I almost gave up, Twig-girl. I helped Darian and Ben with supplies, with advice, so they could tend to the island's herd. But mostly I gave up. I told myself it was because of this." He thumped his palm on his artificial leg. "But that was just an excuse. And who do you think made me realize what I was doing—what I *wasn't* doing?"

Twig blinked up at him.

"It was you, my girl. You gave me the push I needed to keep from staying a useless old man with my best days behind me. You can do the same for Ben."

Twig thought of Mom. Mom, who'd done what she was going to do no matter how Twig had persuaded, pleaded, cried. "Sometimes people won't see."

"In time they all see, Twig. Just, for some, they see too late. Let's hope Ben doesn't make that mistake."

CHAPTER 13

THE AIR SMELLED STRANGE, even for Terracornus. The ground grew muddier, and moss and lichen crawled along the branches of the leafy trees like it did on the evergreens of Lonehorn Island. The air had changed too, but there was no tinge of salt or fresh, rainlike fragrance. The crisp, spicy scent of the silver-green forest gave way to a very different smell. Twig crinkled her nose. It smelled wet—the wet of rotting.

Emmie circled higher, farther from the murky air. In the distance, there was a *pop, hiss*. A burbling, like a pot boiling over.

"What was that?"

"Swamp gas. Wonder's leading us toward the swamp."

The swamp? Twig's heart fluttered with panic. She could hear Casey's voice, lowered for dramatic effect. *Of course there's things alive in the Death Swamp…things that'll make sure you don't make it out alive.*

"Indy went into the swamp?" Twig said. "Why would the thief take him in there?"

"Could be he just came close."

"Or maybe Indy got away!"

"We'll see."

Soon the mud was up almost to Rain Cloud's knees. The trees weren't rooted in the ground; they appeared to be floating—in swamp water. A layer of rich, foamy green carpeted that water.

This was it. The edge of the swamp.

Wonder picked up a hoof even more slowly than usual, and the mud sucked in protest as the swamp tried to cling to her, to hold her back.

"Well, it doesn't look so bad," Twig said hopefully. The water was stinky but not unbearable. It certainly wasn't black. Maybe those stories were just stories, embellished to frighten and thrill. But the look Ben gave her squashed that hope.

He pointed into the vines. Dangling among the bright green was an even brighter rope. It moved, in spite of the absence of a breeze. A snake.

"Poisonous. But this is just the outer edge of the swamp. Farther in, there are other snakes. Other dangers. It's dark. The creatures blend in. People don't see them until it's too late."

"The stories…"

"They're true. We have to turn around."

What about Indy? One look at Ben's face, and Twig swallowed back the words. If Indy was in that swamp…

"The swamp swallows up all other scents. All the water…
its own smells…"

The chances of finding Indy in there were next to nothing.
And the chances of never finding their way out of the Death
Swamp were very high.

With an aching heart, Twig urged Wonder to turn around.
Wonder cried out mournfully, as though she too thought that
the brave Indigo Independence, her father, was lost.

"What now?" Twig asked, looking into Ben's grim face.
"Are we going back to Merrill?"

"No." Ben sighed and stared determinedly into the distance.
"We're going to the castle."

• • •

Ben urged Rain Cloud into a gallop. He knew what he had to
do to save Indy.

"The castle!" Twig gasped. "To see the queen?"

The queen wouldn't see them if he could help it. "The queen
has a library. There's a map of the swamp there. It's our only hope
of finding Indy in there and making it out alive." *Even if Indy
isn't.* Ben tried not to picture him sinking into the mud, deeper
and deeper, not to imagine the swamp lizards gliding through
the water, his desperate cries for help igniting their hunger.

He had to get that map and hope it wasn't too late. Ben

whispered words of encouragement to Rain Cloud. The pony panted after Wonder, who'd begun to toss her head frantically as Twig pushed her on, away from Indy's scent.

Through the trees ahead, Ben spotted something—the telltale pale blur of a unicorn!

"Indy!" Twig cried.

The breeze shifted the branches, and sunlight glinted on something deep gold. The unicorn's trappings were gold and green, the colors of the army of Eastland.

"They're Eastlanders!" Ben said.

But his warning came too late. With a determined leap, Twig and Wonder were off, headed straight for the encampment of Eastland soldiers, dressed in the trappings of a messenger of the Queen of Westland, Eastland's sworn enemy. There was nothing for Ben to do but follow.

Ben heard the cries of surprise, the pounding of hooves, the ring of steel. He was still too far away to help Twig. Ben struggled to ride the unfamiliar pony while readying his bow. Rain Cloud's every response was slow motion compared with Indy, making it even harder for Ben to know whether his subtle signals had been missed entirely.

Though he wanted to rush in, Ben had no choice but to slow Rain Cloud as he approached the perimeter of the clearing. Half a dozen soldiers formed a line in front of him, bows trained on him.

He was outmatched. Ben carefully lowered his bow. Rain Cloud trembled. "We are messengers of the Queen of Westland," Ben said quickly. "My companion's mount is young and…ill. She caught a scent and rushed after it. We come with no intent to harm. We didn't mean to startle you."

"More like distract us," one of the soldiers muttered. He spat on the ground and scanned the forest behind Ben, searching for others.

"Come now, Ackley," the soldier next to him said. "There is the truce. Perhaps the Westlander is telling the truth."

"Westlanders telling the truth?" Ackley sniffed.

"I beg your pardon, sir," Ben said, "but this is Westland. It is you who are guests here."

"That's right. We are Her Majesty's guests, come at her invitation to attend the grand tournament. As a gesture of goodwill. And to discuss matters of great importance. Matters that could affect our truce."

Stolen unicorns. War.

"Perhaps her will is not so good if we are unable to travel under the protection of her invitation, Barlow," Ackley snarled.

A high cry pierced the sounds of chaos coming from the Eastlanders' camp. Wonder. What were they doing to her? What about Twig?

The one called Barlow nodded. "The prince will not be pleased."

"Excuse me," Ben said, "the prince?"

"Reynald. The Prince of Eastland. The one they call—"

"The Boy King," Ben finished for Barlow.

"That's the one," Barlow said proudly.

Reynald was a famous rider and fighter. His unshakable stallion, Stone Heart, was just as famous. With his elderly father ailing and too weak to travel, it was Prince Reynald who represented his people. From here to the farthest reaches of the Barrenlands, Reynald was known as the Boy King. What had started out as a term of derision—mocking a young boy too full of himself, as well as a jab at the true ruler of Eastland—was now spoken with a trace of awe, even by those who despised Eastland the most.

Reynald was not only skilled and intelligent, but he was also ruthless. He had to be. The Eastlanders weren't known to value mercy, and with his uncle vying to take the throne from his ailing father, the young prince had to show his people that he was a king in the making—a king worth waiting for. And he was here, just on the other side of those trees—with Twig, who'd just barged into his camp.

• • •

Wonder leaped over the underbrush and into a clearing full of tents, armed men and women, and more unicorns than Twig had ever seen in once place—unicorns that hardly seemed like unicorns at all. Not like Wonder and Indy, and not like Dagger and the wild herd either. Their bodies were the same, their movement only slightly changed by their armor, but their eyes! They were dull gray instead of swirling with quicksilver life.

"Stop her!" a soldier shouted.

"To the perimeter!"

"It's a trap!"

"Please!" Twig cried. "Don't shoot! It's just a mistake."

But was it? Was Indy here?

Wonder reared and kicked over a cooking pot. Its contents splashed into the campfire. A tower of steam billowed up, and their pursuers backed off. Wonder bounded off again and came face-to-face with the horn of an Eastland unicorn. The unicorn charged with a cold determination. Wonder shrieked at her own hornless state, dodged, and reared again. Could she fight with nothing but hooves and teeth?

Wonder charged at one of the tents with a sense of purpose that defied every warning and plea from her rider. Wonder scraped her head against a tent pole, trying to dislodge her horn cap. The horn cap flipped up—just enough to relieve the downward pressure on her horn for an instant. And an instant was all it took for the point of her horn to rise and push its way out.

Now armed and ready, Wonder turned again to fight. A small, orange-feathered object whizzed through the air. The Eastlanders were done with restraint. Someone had fired. Twig felt Wonder flinch, then the muscles relax underneath her. The strength, the energy, seeped out of Wonder.

The unicorn crumpled, spilling Twig onto the trampled earth. Twig jumped up, drew her sword, and glared at the circle of mounted soldiers around her. Their confusion and concern turned to amusement.

How dare they laugh! Fighting angry tears, Twig turned to Wonder. A tuft of orange feathers fanned out from her perfect white flank.

"No!" Twig dropped her sword and fell to her knees.

"It's just a sleep inducer. She'll be fine in a few minutes. You, on the other hand…" The soldier chuckled. He nodded at two men behind him.

Rough hands grabbed Twig's collar and hauled her to her feet. Twig stared into a shrewd, battle-scarred face.

"Your unicorn gave you away." He kept a tight grip on her as he spoke. His voice was low and raspy. "The queen would never waste such a well-built young mare on a messenger."

"Could be she sent this 'messenger' on her supposedly harmless mount to attack the prince once we let her into our camp," a skinny young soldier said.

"Why would I go barging in like this then? That doesn't make any sense."

"'Cause you're just a girl, and a lousy rider at that," the skinny one replied.

Twig bristled and wanted to say something smart back, but tears pricked her eyes; the burn of a cry tried to make its way up her throat.

"Yes," said Raspy Voice, "but why would the queen send an inferior rider to penetrate our camp?"

Another soldier approached. "Ackley." Raspy Voice nodded at him.

"Looks like there's just the two of them, her and a boy. Quite a bit bigger, but riding a runty horse." Ackley leaned to Raspy Voice's ear, and Twig barely caught his whisper. "He insists on having a word with the prince, alone. He's certain the prince will want to see him."

•••

Ackley tossed Ben's weapons into a heap.

"This way," Barlow said. "To the prince."

Ben followed him to the largest tent, positioned in the center of the camp. Inside, the Boy King sat in a cushioned, gilded chair, his arms crossed, green cape trimmed with braid—not dyed but made of real gold thread.

"So, I have a visitor?" His voice was high—surprisingly boyish. "Interesting, since I've already received a message from the queen today." He rose and strode over to a desk in the corner of the tent, picked up a rolled-up paper, and cast it to the ground with a flourish. "First an insult, a threat to war, even as I journey to the castle at the queen's request. And now this—invasion. You are no messenger of the queen, are you?"

Ben bowed deeply, though it pained him to do it. "No, Your Highness." He couldn't let the Boy King think this was a gesture of war. "But I assure you, we're not—"

"Spies? Assassins? I *will* find out who you are, and there *will* be war! Make no mistake about that. Thievery! Low-down thievery! That's what she's accused me of. How would I steal a unicorn out of her own stable, when I was five days' travel away at the time, you tell me that!"

No doubt the queen thought it had been a professional hired by the ruler of Eastland, perhaps to diminish Westland's forces and to bolster their own, or perhaps just to mock her. If the rumors, and the queen, were right, that meant that someone with access to the key to the passage, with knowledge of its location, had passed these on to Westland's enemies. Someone had ventured all the way into the Earth Land in order to help provoke this war.

Reynald gestured for Ben to rise. He leaned in, just inches from Ben's face. "Soon enough, I'll prove myself against Westland's riders. There will be none who can match me!"

"You *are* a champion of tournaments." Though Ben would've resorted to flattery if that was what it took to get them out of here alive, his statement was true.

"I am a champion of nearly every test of skill! All but the battlefield."

Reynald was too young for a real battle against men; he wasn't much older than Ben. Was he foolish enough to try? Was his father weak enough to allow it? How many men and women, how many unicorns, would die for his desire to engineer his own honor?

Ben looked the Boy King in the eye. He was not going to let that happen. He was going to have to tell him exactly who he was.

•••

Reynald drummed his fingers on the arm of his chair, staring at Ben, now seated in the simpler cushioned chair the Boy King had offered him.

"Ben of the Island. I always hoped we would meet. I never supposed it would be under such…interesting circumstances. My men told me you arrived on a runty old horse. Quite a step down for the son of Darian. I suppose the two of you haven't managed to rein in any of the wild savages on that island after all. So much for the mighty ambitions of Westland's most ardent herders."

"My unicorn," Ben ground out the words, "was stolen. Perhaps you could tell me something about that."

"How, in the name of all the unicorns, do you think I could know you were coming back to Westland and send someone to steal your unicorn as you journeyed?"

Ben laughed humorlessly. "You didn't have to know any such thing, since Indy wasn't stolen from Terracornus!"

"Your unicorn was stolen from the island? You're suggesting I have a whole band of thieves, one of whom I had sail all the way to the Earth Land?"

Ben struggled to hide his surprise. Few Terracornians knew how to get to the Earth Land. Only a handful of Westlanders, as far as Ben knew. It was a relief to know the Eastlanders hadn't figured it out. But if Reynald's ignorance—and his surprise at hearing Indy was taken from the Earth Land—was genuine, then he couldn't be behind the thefts. If not Reynald, then who?

Ben shrugged, hiding his true thoughts. "You're a man of many resources."

Reynald got up and paced across the tent. Abruptly, he spun on Ben. "No one knows you're here. I could kill you right now, and no one would know. I ought to, for such baseless insults!"

Ben wanted to smack the smirk right off his face. Instead he stood and smiled back. "Do you really think I'd travel with just one companion? That no one knows I'm here?"

Ben watched Reynald's doubt grow. He would never guess that only an old herder knew where Ben was, and that even he had no idea exactly where Indy's scent had led him. The Boy King couldn't risk it. If word got out that he'd killed Ben on Westland soil, Reynald would never make it out of the country alive. He'd get the war he seemed to crave, but he'd be in his grave, and it would be his uncle fighting for glory instead, and no doubt taking the crown from the grieving King of Eastland.

"I'm on my way to the castle right now. It's a surprise. I'd appreciate your keeping our little run-in quiet. Your men don't need to know who I am either."

"Why should I care about that? And why exactly are you here? Dressed like that?"

"I didn't want to draw attention to myself." Reynald snorted a laugh, but Ben ignored it. "I've been tracking a stolen unicorn. If the subject comes up, I'd hate to have to tell the queen his scent led me to you."

Anger and fear flashed in Reynald's eyes. Maybe Ben had played his cards right. Maybe Reynald wasn't quite ready to declare war. At least, not until he was safely out of Westland.

Chapter 14

TWIG BLINKED AT THE midday sunlight. The forest opened up to a grassy expanse. Emmie darted out of the trees and into the open sky. In the distance, atop a lone hill, the castle loomed. Its banners rippled, flamelike red and yellow, against a bright blue sky. A broad road led through the open grass to a dark circle of stone around the base of the hill—a massive wall. Behind the wall, chimneys puffed with smoke and the peaks of roofs formed zigzaggy rings.

Ben had cleared things up with the Eastlanders, and they'd served Twig and Ben a nice meal while Rain Cloud rested and Wonder recovered her senses. Then they'd headed out on their own and journeyed through the night, only stopping to doze for an hour or two.

"Herder's Fort." Ben nodded at the castle. "That's what it was called before it was a city, what it was called for hundreds of years. Now the fort is a true castle, and it's called Royal City. Come on. To the road." Ben's words were tight and tense.

With every one of Wonder's hoofsteps on the good, firm

ground, Twig imagined the muck sucking hungrily at Indy's feet. *Hold on, Indy. Please be safe. Let us find you safe.*

As they neared the road, blobs of color slowly moving toward the wall sharpened and became groups of people, some driving large, sturdy, ox-driven carts, others riding donkeys, more straggling on foot.

"Are they all going to the castle?"

Ben pointed at a purple blur in the distance. "That banner above the main gate means it's a tournament day. They're headed to the competition grounds to watch the unicorns and their riders."

"Ben, Merrill told me Wonder chose me to be her rider because she trusted me. What about those riders? What about all the unicorns here and in Eastland?"

"There are other ways. Ways to break them." Ben ducked his face downward. He rode briskly onto the road, into the stream of people.

Twig bit back the rest of her questions. As they neared the wall, the stream of travelers slowed to a standstill and formed a line on each side of the gate, where a couple guards stood, looking people over, occasionally questioning, then giving a nod toward the gate. Their swords were sheathed at their hips, but each of them held a long, heavy stick in his hand.

They approached a guard, and his stick swung down, right between Twig and Ben, right in front of Wonder. Wonder snorted and tried to lunge, but Twig sternly held her back.

"Hold on there," the guard said in a low voice.

Ben said, "She's with me."

The guard held the stick steady right in front of Twig. He gestured at Ben. Ben held an empty hand out and brought Rain Cloud closer to him. He tipped his head up and looked the man right in his face. An expression of recognition and surprise washed over the guard. He made a stuttering attempt at movement, but Ben whispered something that stopped him.

The guard hesitated, then nodded and withdrew his stick. Wonder stuck her nose up in the air as if to say, *Ha! So there.* Twig hurried her through the gate with Ben. "What just happened?"

"I got you through the gate, that's what happened. Just be quiet and come on. He knows my face, from a long time ago. He thinks I'm going to see the queen."

"Aren't we?"

"We're going to take that map."

"Do you mean we're going to *steal* it?"

With a snap of the reins, Ben turned away. "Yah, Rain Cloud. Let's go!"

Twig's stomach tightened. Wonder sensed it and neighed her concern. "It's all right, girl. It's going to be all right." Twig stroked her neck as they followed Ben.

The road circled around the interior of the city wall, past

the stone-walled shops that lined it and to a large expanse of
lawn where dingy tents were pitched.

Beyond the scattered gray-white tents was a tighter, neater
circle of larger tents, their fabric dyed a more respectable tawny
color. And past those, the tops of bigger, brighter tents—red
and blue and gold and green points—stuck up like the angles
of cut gems.

"Those are the tents of the prize riders, the ones who are
competing today."

The crowd thickened with each layer of tents Twig and Ben
worked their way through, until it became an unmoving mass
that formed around some spectacle Twig couldn't quite see.
Ben dismounted, and Twig did the same. She gave Wonder a
short lead. All along one side, elevated on an elaborately painted
wooden platform, were seats. Twig strained to get a better look
at who was sitting there. She bumped right into a young woman,
hurrying by with a barefoot little child clinging to her back.

"Sorry," Twig mumbled.

The child crinkled his nose at her and the woman gave
Twig a perplexed look.

A greasy man shoved a greasier leg of what looked like a bird
right in Twig's face. "Five coppers! Only five coppers."

It smelled good, and Twig's stomach growled, but the grimy
fingers grasping it were enough to convince her to refuse, even
if she'd had five coppers—whatever those were.

"Um, no thanks."

Again, she got a strange look in return.

Ben motioned her away. "Your accent, Twig. Don't talk to anyone. You sound like a foreigner, but you're dressed as a royal messenger."

"Sorry. Shouldn't we be heading for the castle?" she whispered.

"We are. We just need a safe place to leave these two while we get that map."

"I can't leave Wonder here! Can't you get the map by yourself?"

"I cannot leave *you* out here. Don't worry. Merrill's nephew, Pete, is here. He'll keep an eye on them. We just have to find him."

"Why didn't you have Emmie send him a message?"

"It would've drawn too much attention at the castle, and the message could've ended up in the wrong hands."

"Where'd Emmie go, anyway?" Twig scanned the sky until she saw the familiar bright green blur of wings. Emmie settled atop the highest of the wooden platforms, a square-walled red tent in the center of the two largest enclosures.

Ben stiffened. "There's the queen, watching the tournament. This is just a warm-up before Prince Reynald's arrival. She'll put on an even bigger show for her guests. One that shows off the skill of her riders, the quality of her unicorns."

Though the long side of the red, tentlike viewing platform

was open, from her angle, Twig could catch only glimpses of the brightly clothed figures inside.

"Here." Ben shoved Rain Cloud's lead into her hands. "I see Pete. I'll be right back."

Ben strode toward the gem-colored tents. Twig stood there and wondered if she should follow him whether he liked it or not. She was just about to run after him when a tall young man wearing a bright red uniform stepped in front of him. On their journey here, Ben had explained to her that these men were royal guards. He'd told her to avoid them, and now he'd been stopped by one of them.

Ben pointed, and the guard looked right at Twig. She stuffed her hands in her pockets and tried not to look guilty. The guard began working his way away from the tents. Ben waved Twig over, then began following the guard at a distance. Twig tried to read his face for signs of warning. She didn't know what else to do, so she ran to Ben, bringing the pony and the unicorn with her at a trot, hoping they weren't caught.

"Slow down," Ben whispered. "Just look casual."

"What are we doing?"

"That's Pete." Ben nodded at the guard, who was moving briskly through the crowd, out of the tournament grounds. "He's going to slip Wonder and Rain Cloud into the messengers' stables."

"Merrill's nephew is a royal guard? But, Ben, how do you know whose side he's on?"

"I know Pete. Don't worry. Not everyone around the queen is willing to turn me—or any unicorns—in."

He took Rain Cloud's lead, grabbed Twig's sleeve, and tugged her along with him.

Wonder began to toss her head and snort, kicking up dust and clumps of trampled grass, drawing stares. Twig tried to calm her, but she leaped so suddenly, so high, Twig launched up in the air, then thumped down and skidded across her belly, right into a wooden fence. Wonder's lead bit into Twig's hand, but she refused to let go. She coughed out a mouthful of dust.

Right on the other side of the fence, just inches from Twig's nose, a hoof flew, kicking a new cloud of dust right into her face. Twig yelped, then choked. Rain Cloud neighed at Wonder, and the tension on her lead eased. Ben grabbed Twig by the collar and pulled her up.

As she stood, the crowd roared. At her? No—at the competition area inside the fence. There was a snap-crash, then a unicorn bolted past. Jagged splinters of brightly painted wood protruded from his horn. It looked as though they were jousting, only instead of the riders holding lances, they bore only shields, while the unicorns' horns were fitted with lancelike wooden extensions. The horn's brilliant natural spiral was visible only in the glimpses between the black leather straps that held the remains of the false point in place. The unicorn nimbly dodged first the fallen body of his rider, then the wooden obstacle—similar to the jumps in modern horse races—that had been placed in his path.

Unicorns fighting. That's what had set Wonder off. Rain Cloud nipped a warning at Wonder to stay out of it, then pawed at the ground, looking from Ben to Twig. *Get us out of here*, that look said.

"It's all right, you two," Ben told the animals. "We'll be on our way now."

He offered a fold of his tunic to Twig. He pointed at her face. Twig stood there, motionless, staring at the dry, broken ground on the other side of the barrier. There was blood in that dust.

The victorious pair danced around their remaining obstacles, to the finish line. The unicorn raised a pair of hooves, painted to match his rider's colors, and his rider held on tight with one hand and pumped the other up in a fist of mail before the crowd.

Ben wiped the dirt from Twig's face himself. Twig wanted to hide her face in his tunic, to shield her eyes forever from the violent spectacle. She caught Ben's arm as he pulled away.

"Does Indy know how to do that? What if the unicorn thief still has him? Is he going to—"

"That's how it is when men use unicorns to fight their

battles. And even this is just a game, nothing compared to real battle. I don't think a thief would take him into the Death Swamp. Indy must've gotten away. Either way, we have to find him, fast."

Twig reached for Wonder's horn cap. It was still in place—for now. She could feel the pressure of Wonder's horn underneath it, making the metal bulge. She slipped her arm around Wonder's neck and whispered calmly.

Twig looked up at Ben. "We'll find Indy."

Ben just nodded. "We'd better catch up with Pete."

• • •

Pete had Merrill's eyes. Eyes that tempted Twig to trust him. But this was her Wonder Light, her unicorn.

And Ben's unicorn was still missing, probably trapped in the Death Swamp. Twig took a deep breath and handed Wonder over to Pete. She tossed her head at him and bared her teeth.

But Rain Cloud had already decided Pete knew how to behave himself around animals. He whickered at Wonder, calming her down.

"Just make sure you keep them together," Twig said.

"I'll take good care of these two. They'll be right here waiting for you." Pete closed the stall door. The pony and the unicorn were together, in the back of the half-empty messengers' stable.

"We won't be long," Ben said. "Come on, Twig. We'd better go. They just announced the final joust. The queen always hosts a banquet after the tournament. The kitchen will be busy right now. That's where we're going to try to get in, while they're distracted and preoccupied with the preparations."

Twig's stomach growled, and she wrapped her arms around it. "Will we get to eat at this banquet?"

Ben rolled his eyes at Twig.

"Could be it's not such a bad idea, going to that banquet," Pete said hopefully.

Ben shook his head. "Not you too. We're not going to any banquet. I'm here for a map, not to play diplomat."

CHAPTER 15

TWIG FOLLOWED CLOSE BEHIND Ben. He wove expertly through the narrow streets, into an alley piled high along both sides with barrels and crates. Shouts and smells billowed from an open doorway—bread and spices, meat and garbage, laughter and scolding.

"This is the back door to one of the castle kitchens. Just smile and wave if anyone looks," Ben said.

Dead birds and pigs hung from the ceiling on one side of the room. Twig's smile froze on her face. Stomach churning, she focused on the chop-chop-chopping of a hefty cook. At the cook's elbow, a pile of diced onions grew bigger with every chop. A young girl scooped the onion bits into a wooden bowl. The cooks and their helpers seemed too focused on their work to really look at Twig and Ben.

When they'd made their way through the kitchen, Ben opened another door, and they entered a bare stone hallway. From the sound and smell of things, the doors along that corridor led to other kitchens and storerooms.

They wound their way past a steamy laundry and climbed a narrow stone stairway. Ben opened the door at the top, and they entered an empty corridor, constructed of much finer stone and covered with a long strip of dark blue carpet.

"You know where we're going?"

"Of course. Don't worry."

Muffled footsteps sounded on the carpeted stone floor behind them. Twig grabbed Ben's arm.

"Quick!" He flung open the nearest door and pulled her in, then pushed it shut just as a shadow passed by in the corridor outside.

The door was still open a crack; if Ben had latched it just then, whoever was out there would've heard it for sure. Twig shrank back against the wall. It was covered with brightly painted bookshelves. Ben leaned into the wall on the other side of the door.

The shadow disappeared. Twig reached out and put her hand on the door. She eyed Ben questioningly. In or out?

He mouthed, "Shut it."

Twig pushed the door, as quietly as she could, until it latched.

They stood there a moment longer, then Ben let out a long breath.

"Are we okay here or what?" Twig said.

"We're fine. This is the library." Contrary to his words, Ben looked pale with nerves—as though he might even be making a great effort at keeping whatever was left of the meal the Eastlanders had fed them from coming up.

Ben turned his back on Twig and strode past rows of books to a wall covered with wooden cubbyholes. In those cubbyholes were rolls of paper, most of them coated with dust and discolored with age. Maps.

Ben scanned the rows of maps. A large globe mounted on a polished wooden pedestal caught Twig's eye. She spun it slowly on its axis. A hand-painted green mass was surrounded by watery waves of blue. "It doesn't look like Earth."

Ben looked over his shoulder. "It isn't. It's Terracornus."

"There's even more water here than there is on Earth, compared to the land."

Ben shrugged. "It's only a guess. So little of Terracornus has been explored. We only know it's round," he said, giving the globe a swift spin, "because of what we know about the Earth Land. We have some books from when people first came here. We also have some books my great-grandfather brought here."

"Edward Murley?"

Ben nodded. "We have diagrams of telescopes but no telescopes. Books but no printing presses…"

"Or computers."

"No computers. Not even close. Things are always changing in the Earth Land, and they change so fast."

"They don't change much here?"

"Not really. Not until a few years before I was born. The things that have changed since—they seem fast. But I'll bet they're not, compared to the Earth Land."

Twig turned the globe slowly, running her hand over its painted surface. She paused on a small blob of land, which she'd assumed was part of Terracornus. It was separated from Terracornus by a strip of water. Painted in all capitals right across the middle were the words *Earth Land*.

"*That's* the Earth Land?"

"People have come to think that all there is to the Earth Land—to Earth—is the island. They know there's an island, and they know there's a passage. And so they think the passage to the Earth Land is a sea passage. They know that their ancestors used to live there, and so did the unicorns, but they don't believe Earth is another world."

Twig laughed softly. "Who would believe that? And who would believe the passage is a door in a tree trunk?"

"Exactly. A world that's beside ours and yet not really near it? Terracornians don't have any easier a time imagining that than you did before you saw it."

"And no one has explored that far?" Twig pointed to the part of the globe labeled *Earth Land* again.

"We don't have true ships here, only small fishing vessels that hug the coast, so no one has the chance to find out any different."

"But the unicorn thief—he found the passage and a key."

"Yes, he did." Ben frowned as he rubbed a finger over a dusty engraved label below one of the cubbyholes. "Ah! Here it is!" He drew out a roll of paper tied with a black ribbon. "Help me unroll it, just to make sure."

Twig held the map while he plucked at the ribbon. Ben unrolled the map a few inches, then rolled it right back up, satisfied.

Twig wanted to see it, but she knew they were in a hurry.

"Now all we have to do is slip out of here, just the way we came." Ben retied the ribbon while Twig held the map closed.

Sneak out. Just like the unicorn thief. The reminder of what they were doing hit Twig in the gut. "Ben, wait. We can't just take it. It's—stealing."

"It isn't stealing. You don't understand."

"Can't we just ask for it? If we explain why we need it—"

"I shouldn't have to explain anything!" Ben reached for the map, but Twig ducked away, behind the globe.

Footsteps sounded in the hall. They stopped right outside the door. Twig darted across the room as the door handle began to turn. There was a heavy desk there that she could hide under—but the door opened before she could dive down.

A grim-faced castle guard met Twig's gaze. "What's going on here?"

Twig looked from the guard to the map in her hands and back again. She saw it in his eyes—*thief!*

She dropped the map. Ben snatched it up. He tucked his

too-long hair behind his ears and looked the guard straight in the face. Something else registered in the guard's eyes.

"You!"

"We're here to see the queen," Ben said smoothly.

What?

"Oh, you're going to the queen all right, like it or not!" The guard's lip curled up a little, like he wanted to sneer. Or knock the stuffing out of both of them.

CHAPTER 16

EVERY PART OF BEN wanted to grab Twig and run, but that would get them nowhere. They were trapped. He could only hope that if he handled things right, it wouldn't be for too long, and it wouldn't be too late for Indy.

"Fine," he said. "Come on, Twig."

The guard grunted. Ben was pretty sure he was buying his act, but Twig wasn't. Ben gripped her sleeve harder than he wanted to. She looked ready to bolt. If he thought she could make it out of here, he'd let her go and grab Wonder and Rain Cloud and save herself.

Ben tucked the map into the back of his pants, under his tunic. He hesitated, then tore off the tunic. His cloak was in Rain Cloud's saddlebag, and he didn't feel quite himself without it, but at least he could get rid of this ridiculous disguise.

Twig frowned at him, then removed her tunic too. The guard snatched up the discarded garments—evidence of their sneaking. While he was bending down, Ben untucked his shirt and pulled it over the map.

Even free of the tunic, a stream of sweat trickled down Ben's neck. They were about to enter the queen's banquet room, where she and her courtiers would be entertained by singers, storytellers, and jugglers while they waited for the feast. It was sure to be an entrance Her Majesty would never forget.

•••

The floor of the queen's banquet room was covered with something strawlike that Twig couldn't identify. Lighthearted chatter, with a pronounced lilting accent, filled the room. The voices erupted in laughter. A boy in brightly striped clothes tumbled to the floor, followed by a series of colorful balls. One stayed balanced, spinning on his nose. The strangely, richly dressed people assembled around the table applauded the jester.

A woman sat at the head of that table, smiling thinly, eyes gleaming with self-importance. Twig knew at once that she must be the queen. Her light brown hair was swept up in an elaborate style of braids woven through with colored ribbon and held in place with beaded silver pins. Here and there a small, brightly dyed feather was poked artfully through the piles of hair. The other ladies around the table wore similar hairstyles, only less high and less ornate.

The men were dressed in pants and shirts similar to those Ben wore, only they were looser fitting and brightly colored.

Ben stuck out clearly as a boy of the woods and the fields, they as men of the castle—men of prowess, maybe, for most of them looked very strong and a couple had faces that were scarred—but men who, at least today, were dressed for show.

The first to look up at Twig and Ben was a young man, still in his teens, sitting at the right hand of the queen. He jolted a little, and his lips parted as though he were going to speak, but then he put a hand on the queen's arm instead.

The young man must be some royal relative. His chair was nearly as big and elaborately carved as the queen's, and when he touched her, she responded with a look of easy familiarity. A couple of the others regarded Twig and Ben, one with blatant curiosity, the other with an expression of perplexity and disdain.

The young man whispered to the queen, and she looked right at Twig and Ben.

"Ben," she said in a tight, tense voice. Just *Ben*.

The clown stood up. The spinning ball fell from his nose. The queen signaled to the corner, and a bulky figure Twig hadn't noticed before stepped out of the shadows and strode over to her. He scooted her chair back for her as she stood. There were murmurs as Ben made his way toward the head of the table. Twig wanted to run, but she stumbled after him.

"Your Majesty," Ben said right away, without a bow, without a greeting.

"So." The queen waved her hand casually, but a little quaver in her voice betrayed the truth that Ben's appearance meant something to her. "You've finally come. I suppose I shouldn't be surprised you came without your father." Her tone sharpened with anger. "Does Darian know you're here?"

Twig held her breath. She wanted to drag Ben out of here. Away from this woman whose eyes were now burning with contempt.

Ben squared his shoulders. "Darian, leader of the herders of Westland," he said, "is dead."

Ben's face had that hardness to it—hardness against the depths of pain that echoed in his eyes. Every time Twig saw it, she found herself missing the man she'd never met.

The queen stiffened too, but hers was the stiffness of shock. The anger vanished, and a small, anguished sound escaped her lips. The young man, who'd risen to the queen's side, gripped her arm.

"We knew it was going to happen, Mother." His voice strained in an effort not to crack. "You did everything you could."

"Yes. And you have been by my side these years, Griffin." The queen forced a smile. "And our young herder is back, unharmed."

Ben took another step forward. "Unharmed, Your Majesty. But not back. I—"

"No? You have not come back to me, Ben of the Island? Not even with such news?"

"No. Nor will I ever. I haven't forgotten my oath."

"Your oath! Perhaps it's time for you to learn a new lesson about allegiance! Guards!"

But the prince—if that was what they called a queen's son here—had already grabbed hold of Ben with one hand. With the other, he drew Ben's dagger and cut the belt from Ben's waist. The belt, bearing Ben's sword, fell to the floor with a muffled clatter. Before she could think, someone drew Twig's sword and cast it aside.

Ben's sword was closer, so Twig dove for it, sending bits of the strawlike stuff flying. She pulled it free of its sheath, but a boot stomped down on the back of her hand. Twig cried out in agony. The hard, heavy heel lifted, and the guard it belonged to kicked the sword away with the toe of his other boot. Bolts of pain streaked through Twig's hand. She couldn't move her fingers. She tried to get up, but now the sharpness of the boot-heel was in the middle of her back. As long as she stayed still, he didn't press any harder, but every slight movement—

"Neal!" Ben commanded. "Let her go!"

Twig heard the ladies at the table gasp, the chairs of the men scrape back; there was stone beneath the straw. Cold, hard stone. They were ready. Ready to do something—to help Twig and Ben or to harm them? How silly. Of course they wouldn't rise against their queen; they were her courtiers. Twig didn't need to understand Terracornus to understand that.

"She is no enemy of the queen!" Ben shouted at the guard. Then he turned to the queen. "What are you doing? She's just a girl!"

"And you," the prince said, tightening his grip on Ben, "are a prince of Westland. Show some respect for your queen. Your *mother*."

His what?

"Neal," the queen said in a voice of commanding calm, "let the child stand."

The boot lifted. Twig scrambled to her feet. She would've sprinted for the door, but she knew that was hopeless, and besides, she couldn't leave Ben here, whether these people were his family or not.

"Come here, child." The queen crooked her long, pale fingers.

Twig approached, holding her now-throbbing hand against her chest. She looked the queen in the face, and the woman seemed just then to realize—or to care—that her royal cheeks were wet with tears. Tears for her lost husband? But why hadn't he been by her side all along? Why wasn't he king?

The queen produced a silk handkerchief from inside the sleeve of her gown and dabbed carefully at her cheeks with it. She slipped it back into her sleeve and gave Twig a strained smile. "What is your name, child?"

"Twig—Your Majesty."

"Twig, may I see your hand?"

Twig hesitated, then extended her injured hand.

"And the other one?"

The queen slipped her palms under Twig's. They were cool and soft. "Such delicate hands. And I'm afraid my faithful Neal has been a bit of a brute in his eagerness to protect me. I do fear he's broken this one."

Neal bowed stiffly. "Your Majesty, forgive me."

She let go of Twig's hands to wave off Neal's apology. "An automatic reaction. She was reaching for a sword. And it's certainly an unexpected situation—a child threatening the queen."

"I wasn't trying to threaten you. I was trying to protect Ben."

"Ah. It is a noble endeavor, to try to protect Ben." The queen glanced at him with a sad smile, and a fresh tear escaped her eye. Ben flushed. His eyes flashed with anger. "I understand completely. You see, that is what I'm trying to do right now."

"At what cost?" Ben said. "Thanks to you, six young girls were put in terrible danger. Twig is one of them. She's from Lonehorn Island."

"That much is obvious," said the boy the queen called Griffin, the boy who was apparently Ben's older brother.

"I've written to you about Dagger. If you had read my letters—"

"I have read your letters, every one. And every one of them only assured me that I am right to—"

"You are right to ignore the Earth Land, the land our ancestors came from, that all unicorns came from?"

"The concerns of that world are no longer your concerns or mine. Let that world deal with them! There are no more guardians of Lonehorn Island! That was my decree three years ago! Ben, I don't know what possessed you to bring a child of the island with you here. But certainly you understand that you cannot be allowed to go back. And neither can she. Priscilla."

"Yes, Your Majesty." A lady in a plain, pale blue dress hurried over.

"See that this girl's hand is tended to before she joins her friend in the dungeon. Neal, away with him. At once!"

Chapter 17

TWIG TRIED TO SETTLE herself in the corner of the cell. She winced. It was impossible to move the rest of herself without moving her hand. The ice had long melted, and the coolness of the minty poultice was no match for the pulsing heat of pain. Twig had never been hurt like this on the outside. She thought of her stepsister, Emily, being lifted into the ambulance after her bike fell apart and she collided with a car, crying out in pain. A broken leg, a broken arm, a concussion. Twig's stepmother, Keely, had sent Twig to live with the Murleys because she thought Twig had rigged Emily's bike to hurt her.

Twig sniffed back a cry. How had this all happened? How had all her hopes for a life with Daddy turned out like this? All those long, dark afternoons she'd spent after school, back when she was living with Mom. She'd been relieved to be at home, to escape the taunting at school, but then she'd felt so hollow and alone there, while Mom was lost in her own little world. Twig had spent those hours thinking about warm socks and hot things to eat, but more often thinking about Daddy. Daddy coming to rescue her.

She would imagine his tires spinning on the gravel, sending it flying in a cloud of dust as he whirled his pickup to a stop. He'd come running up to the porch, stride right over the empty space where one of the steps was supposed to be, and bang on the door—no, he'd just throw it open. Never mind that he wouldn't know Mom had broken the lock to get in there in the first place; no lock could stop him. Twig would run to him, and he'd scoop her up and take her away and they'd be together, just the two of them, until Mom got things straightened out. And then she'd be the old Mom again, and it would be just the three of them.

Instead of Daddy, the police had come. They had broken down the door because they hadn't bothered to just try opening it, and Mom had been too out of it to answer and Twig had been too scared. But then they'd told her Daddy was coming for her. Twig had known then that everything was going to be all right, that she hadn't been a stupid, stupid hoper after all.

But one thing after another had gone wrong. Daddy had a new family—Keely and her kids, Corey and Emily. And Twig was *not* what they were expecting. She wasn't like them. And then Daddy had left her. That was how it had seemed to Twig then. Even though deep down she knew he was doing something good, something honorable, keeping his word and protecting people.

But who was there to protect her?

She'd ended up with the Murleys, and she'd seen a miracle—Wonder's birth. Twig had changed. Things had seemed right again—in some ways righter than they ever had been. She'd known it couldn't last forever, that she couldn't stay there forever.

But now she was in a dungeon. A dungeon! And now there was more to bear than being alone in the darkness; there was the pain of knowing that a friend was stuck in here with her, that more of them could be in danger without her. People who had dared to love her. Beyond reason. Beyond deserving. Beyond even blood. They'd never know what happened to her. And Wonder, her beautiful Wonder Light—she'd be discovered sooner or later. She'd be forced into the queen's army.

"You didn't tell me," she finally said to Ben. He was sitting with his knees drawn up and his back against the wall opposite her.

He raised his head. "I didn't think you'd understand."

"I wouldn't understand?" Twig stared at him hard. Ben knew about her mother. Twig turned her head sharply away from him. She tried not to cry.

"Twig, I'm sorry. I just couldn't say it."

She nodded. *That* she understood.

"I didn't want to be a prince of Westland to you. The queen's son. I wanted to be..."

"Indy's rider. Ben of the Island."

"My father's son." Those words came out quiet as a breath.

No one spoke for a moment. Twig tried to imagine Darian and Ben together, then Ben's whole family together. No matter how she imagined, they didn't seem to *go* together. "Your mom and your brother don't talk like you," she said.

Ben shrugged. "I talk more like my father. Mother doesn't like it."

"Because you sound more like a herder?"

"She thinks it makes us sound foreign. That it reminds people our family hasn't been here as long as the others."

"I don't understand! I don't understand anything about this place!" Twig's words gave way to a sob. She silenced it, but her shoulders still shook.

"I never should have brought you here."

"It's not your fault. I shouldn't have argued with you about the map. Then that guard wouldn't have found us." She should've trusted him. But then, he hadn't trusted her.

"The map belonged to my father. He would've wanted me to take it to find Indy."

"Why is your mother doing this?"

Ben sniffed. He hugged his knees tighter. There was a long silence. Then he tipped his chin up, leaning his head against the wall.

"She loved my father, but then again, could be she didn't love the real him. Not all of him, anyway. He was a great herder, a great leader. The herdsmen elected him year after year. And he was so young when he first took charge. It was her idea to have him installed permanently, not just as a leader, but as a king. He never told me that. He never would."

"How do you know, then?"

"I heard bits of things. Whispers around the castle. She didn't like the danger. Didn't want him hurt or killed. But that wasn't all. She didn't like the risk of another herdsman being chosen over him, of her losing the importance she had as his wife. And she didn't see why he shouldn't be able to rest after all he'd done and still benefit from his work. She pressured him. So did some of his best friends. And he agreed, for a few years."

"But why are the Eastlanders the enemies of Westland?"

"Rival bands of herders, hundreds of years ago. The herders were divided into groups, responsible for certain areas. Each had their own leaders. At first there were just little skirmishes about territory, arguments about different theories on herd management. They'd be settled fairly quickly, but that could only last so long. Soon it became a matter of pride for a division leader to challenge or fight off a rival division. Next came true splits. Divisions chose sides. There was outright war. All sorts of smaller divisions all fighting each other. They started forming alliances."

"Strength in numbers," Twig said.

"Exactly. Eventually we ended up with Eastland and Westland, along with several smaller lands. Eastland has had a king for two hundred years. But Westland was different, or its allied herders tried to be. So there was no king until my father. Once he gave up the throne and rejoined the herders, some of his men used to shake their heads when he wasn't around to hear and say what a pity it was. That he blamed himself, that Westland never would have consented to a kingship if he weren't such a great leader.

"He never forgave himself for convincing them. Not just being who he was as a herder, but standing by while certain friends of his spoke on his behalf and persuaded them. There had always been people who said we needed a king too, in order for our alliance to be strong enough to keep protecting ourselves against the Eastlanders. But people were afraid to have a king—rightly so, my father said. Too much power all in one place. But enough people admired my father, trusted him like no other man."

"Didn't they think about what would happen when he was gone? Didn't they worry who would take his place?"

"They set it up so that a new king would be elected, while the king's closest relative ruled temporarily in his place. When my father left, that person was my mother. He was certain the system would collapse once he left, that if he rejected the whole idea, people would follow his example. He was wrong. Enough people liked the castle life, were used to their roles there. They urged my mother to stay, and they supported her. She proposed a law making the kingship inherited, from my father to Griffin, once he's of age, and they made sure it was passed."

"Why didn't she go with your father?"

Ben didn't say anything.

"She felt like he left her, maybe," Twig said.

He nodded. "At first he was sure she'd change her mind and come join him, and she was just as certain he'd change his mind and come back. But each of them only grew more determined about their own way. Publicly, my mother pretended that my father just wasn't suited to castle life. She acted as though they agreed that he would leave, and she would stay. Some of the herders said that once she did that, once he realized she was going to stay as queen, he didn't have the heart to fight her openly."

"She broke his heart. But...what about you? You ended up with your father. How?"

"I followed him," Ben said as though it were that simple, that obvious.

"How long ago was that?"

"Five years ago, I think."

"You were so little."

"I was too young to have a unicorn of my own, but I knew

how to ride. I took one of the castle unicorns, and I rode hard, trying to catch up with them. I was crying hard too. I couldn't think straight. I couldn't see straight. I lost my way. I was nearly unconscious with thirst, half dangling from the unicorn's back, when my father's men found me. He tried to send one of them back with me, to take me to my mother once I was well, but I escaped every time. Finally my father decided it was less dangerous to keep me with him and raise me as a herder than it was to have to keep rescuing me from the wilderness and the desert."

Twig thought of her own father, in the wilderness now. In the desert. Would she have followed Daddy if she could?

CHAPTER 18

A COUPLE HOURS INTO THEIR confinement, Twig opened her mini-backpack and took out her sketchbook and the new colored pencils Keely had sent her for her thirteenth birthday. She scooted to the front of the cell, closer to the feeble light in the hallway beyond the bars. She opened her sketchbook to the page where she'd tucked her birthday card from Mom. It was just a piece of regular paper, decorated with a hand-drawn heart. A heart, drawn in a jail cell.

Twig flipped the pages to a pencil sketch she'd done of Casey. It was a struggle with only one good hand. Even more of a struggle to stay calm, to not give in to the darkness of the dungeon.

Mrs. Murley said she was getting really good at drawing faces. It was scary, drawing the people she loved. She was always afraid she'd get something wrong. But it made her feel closer to them. Twig shut her eyes, picturing Casey's, big and brown. She opened her eyes and selected several different browns. She would mix them to make just the right color.

Twig jumped at the sound of footsteps. She dropped the pencil, and the fragile tip broke.

A guard opened a little hatch at the bottom of the door and pushed a heavy tray of food through. Ben had his knees drawn up to his chest again. He opened one eye and peeked indifferently to see what was coming through the hatch.

The food wasn't served on a silver platter, but it certainly looked like it came from the royal table. She picked the tray up, winced in pain, then set it down in front of Ben. Twig reached for a pastry with her good hand—her right one—but had to pull back as Ben shoved the tray away. He glared at the food as though it were a bitter enemy and crossed his arms.

"I know you're mad," Twig said, reaching for the pastry again, "and I know you're worried about Indy—I'm worried about Wonder and Rain Cloud too—but we have to eat anyway."

She took a bite, and Ben leaned his head back against the wall. He stared at the seeping stone on the other side of the cell.

Twig swallowed. "Don't you think I'm mad too?"

"I think—" He shifted his gaze toward her. Then, "Never mind."

"What?"

"I think you're softer than I thought."

"Softer than you, you mean. Because I eat when I'm hungry and there's food? Maybe I'm not softer than you. Maybe I'm smarter than you. Did you think of that?"

"They're trying to soften us up, and you're encouraging them!"

Twig snorted a laugh and accidentally blew a cloud of powdered sugar off the top of the pastry, dusting her face.

Ben smiled. Twig ignored him and took another bite. That one got her right to the gooey middle of the pastry. It tasted like coconut pudding. Delicious.

"Who cares whether they're encouraged or not? I'm building up my strength so we can break out of here and get Indy."

Ben laughed out loud at that. "Your strength? You've got quite a bit of building up to do before you can outmatch the royal guards. Better go ahead and eat up then."

"That's not what I meant. I meant—I meant my mental strength."

"Huh," said Ben. "You've got a blob of custard right there." He touched the corner of his mouth.

Twig left the blob there just because he'd pointed it out, and she kept eating in silence and he kept sitting there not eating and pretending not to watch her eating. Still, she was careful to save half of everything for him. A little more than half; he was a little bigger, after all. It only seemed fair. When she was done she wiped off the sugar, licked around her mouth, then rubbed it all the way clean with her finger.

That's when she saw the note, tucked under one of the plates. Twig pulled at the exposed corner. She nudged Ben as she unfolded it. "Look! It's from Pete!"

Ben leaned over her arm and read aloud, "Your mounts have been moved off the palace grounds to a safer place. Both are well. Hope to get you back to them soon."

"They'll let us out of here tomorrow," Ben said in a hopeless tone that was entirely out of step with his words.

"They will?"

"Oh yes. We won't get to see Wonder and Rain Cloud, but Mother will surely offer you more custard pastries once you agree to join her court."

Twig ignored the jab. "Maybe she'll let us go get Indy! Maybe she'll even send someone with us to help!"

"She won't help us get Indy. She doesn't care about Indy. She'll never care."

Ben's eyes glistened with tears. His voice shook. But it was the unmistakable thread of despair that shook Twig. Was he really giving up? Not just on Westland and all its unicorns, but on Indy?

"But couldn't we escape then, Ben?"

"It's just as easy for the castle guards to keep an eye on us at court as it is in the dungeon. How did it feel when that boot broke your hand? How did it feel when you had another boot in your back? Have you forgotten already?"

"Helpless," Twig admitted.

"That's how it is in her court. You're helpless, all the time. There's a boot in your back, all the time, even when there isn't.

Don't you understand? And if we come into court all clean and fat and fed…"

He gestured at Twig with his head, and Twig glanced at herself, and finding her body as skinny as ever—well, not as skinny as ever, since she'd filled out a little bit since coming to the Murleys', but anyway, just as skinny as she'd been when she came to Westland—she glared back at him.

"It's easier for her to pretend I've learned from my father's death and come back to her, for her to use his death as proof she was right. To use it against everything he died for."

"So what's your plan then?"

"I don't know yet. I'm trying to think, but…" He gave Twig a resentful look.

"Great. So your plan is to try to think of a plan. On an empty stomach."

He folded his arms tighter and closed his eyes. Twig scooted the tray back in front of him, got up, and began to examine the room again. She was calmer now, and her stomach was full, and her eyes had adjusted to the semidark. She would see something she hadn't seen before, something that would help them escape. She had to.

•••

The cell door clattered open, and Ben jumped to his feet. Twig yelped.

A hulking figure filled the doorway. "You've been summoned. Dinner, this evening."

Ben gave Neal his hardest stare. "No thanks."

The hands were on Ben's collar as quick as a blink. They twisted his shirt tight around his throat and hefted him up. "No one asked for your opinion! When the queen summons you, you come!" The shout rang in Ben's ears and bounced against the dank cell walls.

Ben ripped at Neal's hands with his. "Get your hands off me. I am a prince of Westland!"

Twig ran at Neal, and he let go with one hand to swat her away. Her feet flew out from underneath her, and she hit the hard floor with an awful thump.

Neal cocked his head at Ben, giving him a little shake with the fist that was still wrapped in his shirt. "A prince of Westland? Are you now?"

Ben swung his fist right at that grin, but Neal caught it in one beefy hand. "You might be a prince of Westland, but she"—he glanced at Twig, scrambling to her feet—"is *nothing*."

Ben's punch was thwarted, but his knee thrust into Neal's gut. It wasn't enough. He hated this. Hated everything that was happening. Hated being helpless to stop it. "Don't you dare call her that! She's my friend and a great rider!"

Neal laughed humorlessly. "It doesn't matter what she is to you. You're nothing either. The queen'll realize that soon enough."

What if Neal was right? She already didn't care about him. She'd washed her hands of him once he'd run away to join his father. No, she cared, in her own twisted way. She'd thrown him in the dungeon, but even that, she'd done to protect him. Or at least to protect herself from losing him. But those were two different things, weren't they?

A new wave of anger surged up in Ben. Why did he care? What kind of herder was he if he wanted someone like the Queen of Westland, enemy to all unicorns and everything he'd sworn to protect, to care for him?

"You're coming to dinner. The Boy King, the Prince of Eastland, has arrived. He's inquired about you. The queen told him you'd be at dinner."

It wouldn't look good for the queen if Ben didn't show up. Reynald might have kept it secret that he'd seen him on his way here, but of course he would expect to see Ben once he got to the castle. Ben had told him he was on his way there, and Reynald had no idea how bad the rift between Ben and the rest of Westland's court was.

If Reynald knew about this weakness in the royal family, it would only make him bolder. Did Ben care about helping his mother maintain her image, her ability to keep the upper hand, her comfort, her power? Would his father want him to do that? Ben wasn't sure.

But if Neal was willing to hurt Twig, it didn't matter. He had no choice. The feeling of helplessness sucked at his insides like swamp mud; it made his stomach churn like the swamp's putrid gasses. He was stuck. Just like Indy.

Ben's hands hung limp at his sides, and Neal let him go.

"You're to come with me now and get dressed in something suitable."

Ben looked at Twig. How could he face his mother, his brother, and Reynald all alone? How could he pretend to be a prince? But how could he refuse to go, and risk Neal hauling Twig off in order to punish him?

Twig lifted her quivering chin up, a determined look in her eye. "Let's go, Ben."

Let's? Ben's heavy heart lightened just a little. Maybe with her beside him he could still be Ben of the Island. Maybe he wouldn't have to pretend—but could Twig handle a royal banquet?

"It's just dinner, right?" Twig said.

Ben struggled to return her wry smile. A banquet with the Prince of Eastland. "Right. Just dinner."

"The queen didn't say nothing about *her*."

"But Reynald did, when we met him on the way here. What if he asks about Twig?"

"Fine." Neal drew his sword and motioned them to go in front of him. He pointed the blade at their backs. "Behave yourselves or the Earth Lander'll get it."

CHAPTER 19

BEN'S OLD ROOM WAS exactly as he'd left it—except that somebody had tidied it up and kept it clean all these years. The same bed with its deep blue comforter, a rich color fit for a prince. A prince he'd never wanted to be. He'd jumped on it like a child of the wilderness. He remembered begging Griffin to join him. But Griffin was too princely to stoop to that level.

His father had stretched out on that bed next to him at night, after his mother had tucked him in and kissed him, when Ben begged him to stay a few more minutes, just the two of them. He'd tell Ben stories about the old days, about herding, about wild unicorns. Stories his mother didn't approve of.

"I want to be a herder like you, Father," Ben would say. Then his father's smile would fade. Sometimes he'd remind Ben, "Your mother used to be a herder too."

Ben always found it hard to believe the stories about his mother herding. They were great stories, but it was like they were about someone else.

"This was your room?" Twig's question was near a whisper, but it startled Ben out of his memories.

"Yes. I haven't been here since I was small. Since I ran away to find my father."

"So…I guess we're supposed to get dressed. Do you think there's any girl's clothes in there?" Twig pointed at the wardrobe. Its doors were painted with twin unicorns, leaping so that their horns touched where the doors met.

Ben opened the wardrobe. Little suits hung there, freshly laundered and perfectly pressed. Had he really been that small? Had his mother really thought he'd stayed that small? More likely she'd simply ordered the maids to keep his room ready when he'd first disappeared, then never given the wardrobe another thought or the maids another direction about it. Ben pushed the child's clothes aside. A new suit of clothes, just his size, hung on the other side. It was far too fancy for his liking, but at least it was green, and not some garishly bright combination that would make him look like a walking flower. But what about Twig?

As if in answer, someone rapped briskly on the door.

"Come in," he said.

Neal stood guard at the door as a young maid entered with a pale blue gown draped over her arm. "For the young lady," she said curtly.

Twig made no move to take the clothes, so Ben swept them

out of the maid's hands. He gave her a good glare for turning her nose up at Twig.

Once they were alone again, Ben pointed to the dressing screen in the corner, a silverwood frame draped in heavy tapestry. "You can change over there, Twig. I'll dress out here."

Putting on those clothes felt like putting on someone else's skin. A false self he'd fought to shed all those years ago. He'd never felt he'd belonged here in the castle. Neither had Darian. He'd always known that. Was that why Ben had felt the same way? Because he was his father's son?

He couldn't stay here. He couldn't see his mother. Or Griffin. He hadn't missed the accusation in his brother's eyes. Griffin blamed Ben for their father's death. And why shouldn't he? If he'd let Indy kill Dagger when he had the chance—

"Ben?" Twig emerged from behind the dressing screen. She smoothed the silk gown with her hands. They were shaking. "I was thinking…I know, it's a little big. I look weird, don't I?"

"No…"

"Anyway—" A stray white feather had found its way from the collar of the gown into her hair. It floated down into her face, and she batted it away. "I don't want you to just go to this banquet for me."

Ben folded his arms across his chest. She had an odd, determined look about her. Whatever she was going to say, he was pretty sure he wasn't going to like it.

Twig pushed on. "Don't just go there to show your face. Go there for Indy. For Westland. For all Terracornus."

She sounded like Merrill again. *Keep your oath and go to the queen.* The words from the thief's note nagged at him. He hadn't vowed to go to her, but he *had* taken an oath to protect unicorns.

"You're still her son. You can influence her. Merrill said you should try to persuade her to make peace with Eastland. To start turning Westland back to what it was."

"I cannot influence the queen."

It was *she* who would influence *him*. She'd try to undo everything his father had raised him to be. He'd seen her face when she'd found out his father had died. "We knew it was going to happen, Mother." That's what Griffin had said. They'd been right. And now Indy was lost. They were his family. He hadn't been prepared for how much seeing them would make him want that. He'd tried not to think about them all these years, other than despising what they were doing to Westland and its unicorns. He'd told himself that was why he couldn't stand to come here.

Twig grabbed his sleeve. "You have to try. I'll be there with you, Ben."

"It's a bad idea. It won't end well."

"And how will it end if we do nothing?"

Ben sank onto the foot of the bed. He picked at the gold

tassel on the corner of the comforter. "You think I'm stronger than my father? He could stand up to them and love them at the same time. I never could. But even he couldn't do it here, after the way my mother changed. I don't think I can—"

"And I thought I couldn't ride a unicorn, remember!"

He remembered. He remembered he'd talked her into it.

Twig gripped the bedpost like she wanted to shake it—and shake him right off the bed. "We're not nothing, Ben. Neither of us. We were made for something."

"I know that! I used to think I knew what that was. My father's partner, Indy's rider, protector of the island's herd. But now—Indy needs me. The island needs me. I don't know if they need me, but the Murleys *want* me. And now you and Merrill are trying to tell me that all of Westland, all the unicorns and people of Terracornus need me. And in their own way, my mother and my brother are trying to tell me they need me, or at least they need me to go along and do whatever they want! I cannot do all those things! I cannot do any of those things, and we're both stuck here!"

He hurled a pillow at the wall, sending a painting of the countryside clattering to the floor.

A tear slipped down Twig's cheek, and Ben regretted his outburst. She was scared. Scared and trying to be brave for him. Twig had every reason to be afraid. His mother had made it clear she didn't want Twig going back to the Earth Land

and telling everyone about the passage, about Terracornus. Ben's mother had married a Murley, a recent descendant of Earth Landers. She knew there was more to the Earth Land than the island—a whole world for Twig to tell about theirs. He took a deep breath, trying to calm down, trying not to feel even more caged in this room and its memories than he had in the dungeon.

Twig didn't stop crying, but she put a hand on Ben's arm. "Just think about one thing at a time. You can't change Terracornus or even Westland all at once, but maybe you can get your mother and the Boy King to agree to keep their truce. Maybe you can convince her to let us out so we can get Indy."

Ben tried not to look as hopeless as he felt. "She used to be different…"

"My mom changed," Twig said softly, hesitantly, "and that changed me. I thought that meant we could never change back. In a way, I was right. Neither of us could ever be exactly the same. But I found out *I* could change. I could be something new. Something stronger. You helped show me that, Ben. You *are* that now. You didn't follow her ways. You found a way out. Westland is more like how I was. Stuck, thinking that from now on, this is how it always has to be. But I'll bet some of them have never stopped dreaming that something would happen, that somebody would come and make everything right again. Even if she doesn't change, that doesn't mean Westland can't."

"It was so easy to know what to do when my father was here. And then, even when he was gone, when it came to the herd, I just had to ask myself what he would do. It wasn't so hard to figure out. But this…"

"I never had that with my dad."

That was hard for Ben to imagine. "Is that why you went with your mom instead of your father?" he asked.

"He was gone for training, for the army. My mom told me we were moving. I didn't know we were moving away from him. I didn't know he didn't know where she was taking me."

"It wasn't your fault, Twig."

Twig shrugged. Neither of them said anything for a long time. Then Ben had to ask, "Twig, do you think she'll ever change?"

"I don't know. But I know…" Twig gulped. She brushed the tears from her cheek. "I know it's not your fault if she doesn't."

"I meant *your* mom."

"Oh."

He gave her a nudge. "The same thing's true for you, then, isn't it?"

"Yeah, I guess it is." She tucked a strand of straggly hair behind her ear.

"They'll send someone to do your hair, I think."

She scrunched her nose. "Will they put feathers in it?"

"Probably."

"I'll look even weirder."

"You'll look like a lady."

And he was going to have to be a prince. It was the only way to do any of the things Twig wanted him to do. The things he felt sure now that he was supposed to do. His mother wouldn't help Ben the herder, Ben the unicorn rider, Ben of the Island. She had turned her back on him a long time ago.

CHAPTER 20

BEN STRODE INTO THE banquet room with his head held
high. Twig followed, but she looked down at her slippered
feet, at the floor. She felt ridiculous, and her hand was throbbing
again. Maybe she should've stayed back in the cell. Ben seemed to
know his way around here well enough. What did he need her for?

"Lift your head up," Ben whispered.

Twig flushed and raised her chin. She'd heard that often
enough from the Murleys, with their gentle but firm ways
of trying to help her be something better, of reminding her
that she was made for something better. But would even the
Murleys expect her to walk into a queen's banquet room with
her head up? Especially with Neal, the queen's guard, herding
them in with his threatening glare.

But she'd just told Ben that he could do this—not just get
through dinner, but really do something, really be who he was.
She'd been so scared talking to him, telling him those things.
But it seemed like he'd listened, like he was going to try. She
couldn't let him down now.

One step into the room, and Twig didn't have to worry about keeping her eyes off her feet—they were fixed on the table. The great, long slab of oak was heaped with platters of food, the air thick with a spicy mix of aromas that made Twig's stomach untwist from its clench of nervousness and growl hungrily.

At the opposite end of the table sat Reynald, the Boy King, flanked by his guards, Ackley and Barlow. Reynald spoke quietly to Ackley. A smile played on his lips. Twig couldn't help but think it looked devious.

"Your Majesty, Prince Griffin, and Prince Reynald of Eastland," announced a young man stationed at the door, "may I present Prince Ben and Twig of Lonehorn Island."

The nonroyals at the table stood. Ben bowed stiffly at his family and Reynald. Twig followed his lead and stumbled into a curtsy. They were shown to their seats, directly across from the queen. Once again, Griffin was seated at his mother's side.

Twig concentrated on eating while the royal family of Westland made small talk with Reynald about his journey from Eastland.

"I hear you ran into my brother along the way," Griffin said to Reynald.

Twig glanced at Ben. His smile looked even more forced than before. She hoped he'd keep his cool and think about what she told him earlier. Now that she was here, facing these people, she didn't know if she'd have the guts to ask the queen for anything either.

"Ye-es," Reynald said. His eyebrows went up in surprise, and Ben's face froze.

Ben had told Twig about how he'd asked Reynald to keep quiet about seeing them. But then, because she'd tried to come along, he'd blurted it out to Neal.

Reynald turned on Ben. "I suppose you've added your own false accusations to fuel your mother's fire. I should've known I couldn't trust anyone from this family to keep his word."

Griffin looked taken aback. He held out his hands in a gesture of peace. "Let's all just stay calm now. I'm sure no one is accusing anyone of anything."

But Ben shouted, "I am a man of my word like my father before me!"

Ackley and Barlow began to rise, but Reynald pushed them back. He barked a laugh. It sounded high, like a yippy little dog. "These two were caught in my camp, disguised as royal messengers. Prince Ben claimed to be tracking a stolen unicorn. He threatened to tell you some made-up story about its scent leading him to my camp."

"Unicorn? What unicorn?" the queen said.

"It's not made up!" Twig said. "Your Majesty, we don't know who this unicorn thief is, but he got through the passage to Lonehorn Island. He took Ben's unicorn, Indy."

"Twig!" Ben cried.

Twig hurried on before Ben could stop her, before she could lose her courage. "We think Indy got away from the thief, and now he's in the Death Swamp. Your Majesty, please, you have to help us find him and then you have to change the lock on the passage door. We'll go back to the island, and I promise I won't tell anyone about this place."

The queen's eyes widened. She regarded Reynald. "You have been trespassing on my island?"

"*Her* island?" Twig whispered to Ben. "I thought she didn't care about the island."

Ben gave her a look. She could tell he was biting back his own outrage not only at Reynald, but at his mother's claim. But Twig thought she understood. They needed the queen to care right now, even if it was only because of her rivalry with Eastland.

"Another false claim!" Reynald said. "And here I've journeyed all this way in order to meet with you and try to prevent war!"

"If the Prince of Eastland wanted to prevent war, he might have instructed his minions not to trespass on my territory, and especially not to steal my best unicorn right out of the castle stables."

"And if the Queen of Westland wanted to prevent war, she might avoid such outrageous accusations!"

Twig could feel the tension rumbling beneath the silence that followed. She'd made a terrible mistake coming here. She didn't understand this place, these people, the way Ben did. Who was she to try to give him advice? She should've known better. *Please*, she prayed. *Do something. Help us.*

• • •

Ben knew what he had to do. Not because he thought it was what his father would want. Certainly not because it was what his mother or brother would want. Not even because it was what he thought Twig or Merrill would want him to do. He'd cried out in his heart for help, for an answer, and now his heart was pounding with the truth. This time it was up to him. *Stand up. Speak up.*

He stood up. He opened his mouth, though he had no idea what to say. "What would be the point of war, Prince Reynald, when you cannot fully participate in it?"

Reynald narrowed his eyes at Ben, studying him.

"I have a proposition for you," Ben said.

"I'm listening."

"A chance to defeat me. A chance to get back at me and at my mother. A chance to prove yourself against a son of Westland. One of comparable age…and the son of the great Darian too." Ben barely managed to keep the emotion out of his voice as he said his father's name. No, as he *used* his father's name. As soon as the words were out of his mouth, Ben wanted to beg his father for forgiveness, to take it back—but then he saw the look on Reynald's face.

The spark of interest had bloomed into full-fledged hunger. Hunger for glory and for Ben's blood.

"Ben!" Twig said. "What are you going to do?"

"I'm going to duel Prince Reynald—not just any duel—a duel of the flags, through the Death Swamp, just as in the old times."

The Boy King said, "The victor will be remembered for generations to come." From the look on his face, he had no doubt he would be that victor. And that was all he cared about. Ben knew this was a dangerous game he was playing. But it just might get Indy back, not to mention put off war with Eastland.

"A *Death Swamp* Duel?" Twig cried.

The same words were murmured around the table. A smattering of applause broke out among the group. But a look from Griffin sent hands back into laps before the queen could take note of who'd dared thrill to such an idea.

"Your son has offered to settle our dispute with a duel," Reynald said. "We are of the same age. As fair a match as Westland can make."

"You are willing to put your life on the line?" Griffin said.

Reynald grinned. "One death instead of thousands. I, too, care for my people and for unicorns."

Ben resisted the urge to roll his eyes.

Griffin threw his chair back and stood over Reynald. "You are a brash little boy and a show-off! You want nothing but to be the one who killed Darian's son, and not in battle, in a public spectacle! It's ridiculous! It's—"

"That's enough, Griffin." Ben moved quickly around the table to stand between them. He turned to Reynald. "As soon as I have my unicorn back, we can proceed with the duel."

"Ben of the Island, you have a deal, but I know nothing about your unicorn. I suppose you'll have to borrow another."

Twig looked ready to dive over the roast duck and across the table. "He couldn't possibly—"

"He couldn't possibly go back on our deal just because he doesn't have his favorite unicorn." Reynald's mouth curled up again, the way Ben hated.

A Death Swamp Duel without Indy? *Everything* without Indy if he didn't get to him soon. He knew Reynald was telling the truth, but it didn't matter. His mother would have to let him search for Indy. She wouldn't want him losing that duel.

"There is no deal. I am Queen of Westland! I have lost my husband over one foolish, outdated notion. I won't lose my son over another. There will be no duel."

"Then there will be war," Reynald said.

"Yes, I'm afraid there will." The queen's words were coated with ice.

"I gave my word!" Had she lost all sense of pride? He'd been counting on that, blast it all! It was all he could ever count on from her. Ben looked Reynald right in the eye. "I will keep it. For the people of Eastland and Westland. For the thousands of unicorns that will die if I don't."

Reynald nodded, an eager gleam in his eye. He and his escorts excused themselves from the table, leaving the Westlanders.

"Ben." His mother said his name so tenderly. Like he was her little boy again. Her eyes brimmed with hurt. He wanted to make it go away. He wanted to make her happy. He took a step closer to her. "Mother, I'm going to find Indy, my unicorn. There is no match for him. Not even Prince Reynald's famous stallion, Stone Heart. You'll see. Everything will be all right."

She shook her head. Her gaze turned cold again. A cold that trickled through Ben's chest, then stuck like a lump of ice, accidentally swallowed.

"Neal," she said, "take them back."

CHAPTER 21

TWIG JOLTED AWAKE. BEN'S outstretched arm was in front of her, holding her back. When she opened her mouth to speak, he clamped his hand over it. She froze.

A slow, soft creak. Then a click. Someone had turned a key in the lock. The cell door eased open, and a bulky figure blocked the flickering of the corridor's torchlight.

"I'm a friend," he whispered. His voice was rough and low. A glimmer of light bounced off a long object in his hand—a sword.

The stranger said, "Let's go."

Ben didn't hesitate. He pulled Twig to her feet, reached for her back to feel that her pack was there, and pulled her toward the door as the stranger eased it open.

Twig's heart kept leaping between relief and fear. It had been a hard night. They were both bruised and battered from their struggle with Neal and the other guards. When he realized his mother was locking them back up, Ben had burst into a fury Twig had never thought possible. Once they were shut in the cell again—tossed there with no more ceremony than the bundle of their own clothes that were hurled after them—he'd fallen apart.

Twig had cried as she slipped her clothes on under the now-tattered gown, then pulled the ridiculous costume off. She wanted Mr. and Mrs. Murley. They knew what to do with people who were falling apart. What did Twig know? She was only half put together herself. Being this new Twig wasn't easy. In the end, she'd cried with Ben and prayed prayers that only seemed to echo off the stone walls and back at her, ever damper and darker, until finally they'd both fallen into a restless sleep.

The stranger glanced back at them as they followed. A flash of firelight illuminated his crooked nose and pale, serious eyes.

"Ben," Twig whispered once the stranger had looked away again. "Isn't he one of the dungeon guards?"

"Of course. How else would we get out of here? Now shh!"

"But—"

"Merrill," Ben said. "It must've been."

Merrill had arranged this? Is that what he thought? Twig didn't know what to think, but they didn't have time to think, not if they were going to get out of here. Where could this man take them that could be worse than the dungeon?

As soon as she asked herself that question, Twig imagined all sorts of nightmarish possibilities. Her imaginings must be far worse, she tried to console herself, than any real possibilities in Terracornus.

Wonder and Rain Cloud were waiting for them somewhere. And somewhere, in the darkness on the other side of the passage door, wild unicorns were waiting for a leader. Without one, they could attack the ranch again. And now Ben and Twig knew that someone else was using the passage. The unicorns could be stolen. The Murleys and the girls could face not only the dangers of wild unicorns, but also strange people from another world.

Would the Murleys venture into the forest in the dark of night, into the territory of the unicorns, into the shadows where strangers lurked, trying to find Twig?

Twig and Ben turned a corner in the narrow dungeon corridor, and their guide stopped to produce a key from around his neck and to unlock an even narrower door.

"Watch your step," he said. And then he took a step himself and disappeared downward, into the blackness beyond.

"Ben!"

"There's a rail," he said gently. "Here." He took her hand and moved it until she felt the cold smoothness of an iron stair rail underneath it. "Got it?"

Twig bit back a gasp of pain. She'd forgotten about her hand. She groped around and gripped the rail on the right side instead. "Yeah. Got it."

"I'm right behind you." Ben sounded like himself again.

The good, solid Ben that she could depend on. He took hold of her hood with his free hand. He wouldn't let her fall.

Ahead of her, footsteps fell carefully, quietly—but heavy just the same—in a steady rhythm, down and down. The stairs were long and black and winding. Twig felt out the edge of each one with the toe of her boot and lowered herself to the next, until she got a sense for their size, their spacing. She took them faster, faster, fast as she dared. But still, she could not help wondering why they were going down, why they seemed to be heading deeper into the castle that had become their prison.

Finally their path leveled out. Twig feared that any moment they'd turn a corner and a door would slam behind them, shutting them into the depths below the castle where no one would see or remember them, and they would never find their way out. Just as the panic was reaching up from her belly into her throat, tempting her to grab Ben and refuse to go any farther, the dank ground began to slope upward. Gently, subtly, but upward—cautiously, like Twig's hope.

The farther they went, the less dank and stale the air became. It was still stuffy in its own way, but its heaviness was earthy, not reeking with the stench of hopeless men; it was wet and cold, but like rained-on soil, not like weeping, seeping stone.

The slope gave way to another set of stairs, this time climbing upward. Ben said, "I think we're on the other side of the wall."

"The city wall?"

"Yes."

"But you don't know?"

"My father told me about a passage. His passage. From the dungeon, underground, across the castle grounds, through the city, under the wall, and into the forest. We're really getting out of here. We're going to find Indy." Ben's voice trembled with excitement.

At the top of the stairs, the passage continued, flat and straight, but dark and narrow as ever. Twig was just considering pulling her flashlight out of her jacket pocket when she noticed a blacker patch of darkness just ahead, on the right side of the tunnel wall. Another passage?

Twig squinted. The blackness seemed to shift. Yes, it moved. Someone was there! Someone was listening to their footsteps, waiting for them to pass by the opening. A cloaked figure drifted out of the other passage and stood across theirs. It reached under its cloak, and Ben reached for his sword—his sword that wasn't there.

Chapter 22

TWIG GRABBED HER FLASHLIGHT and turned it on.

"Easy now," their guide said in his gravelly whisper.

The shadowy figure pulled something out from under his cloak, but it wasn't a sword; it was a little bag, hanging heavy from a drawstring. The bag swayed, and there was a faint musical clink of coins. He said nothing, and neither did their gruff guide, who took the bag of money and stuffed it into a pack at his hip. The flashlight glow revealed several more openings in the passage wall ahead. Twig jerked her flashlight beam from one of them to the other, then back to the cloaked figure.

Her hand trembled, and the light wobbled as she waited and prayed. The figure didn't go away; he stepped past the guard, and he reached for the clasp of his cloak and undid it. His hood fell back, and he pulled the garment the rest of the way off. Twig gasped. It was Griffin.

She glanced frantically at the dark corridors opening up all around them. He'd paid off the rescue Merrill had sent for them. Now what was he going to do with them? Which way should they run?

Ben just said, "Griffin?"

In a swift, fluid motion, Griffin swung the cloak around and draped it over Twig's shoulders. "It's a cool night. This will keep you warm and hidden. Cover those lights on your coat."

"Lights?" Twig uttered in a choked voice.

Ben picked up her arm from under the cloak and tugged at the reflective strips on her sleeves. *Oh. Lights.*

"Hurry now. Your weapons and your mounts are waiting." Griffin turned, and they followed.

"But, Ben," Twig whispered, "should we trust him?"

"Yes."

"You're sure?"

"I'm sure."

"But why? He—"

"He prefers not to have me around, to have our mother to himself. He does what she wishes, and he's her favorite. I can trust him to get rid of me."

"But you were in the dungeon!"

"I told you, she wouldn't have kept me there forever. I'm her son. This way, Griffin gets rid of me before she has a change of heart. Before I have a change of heart. He thinks I'm going to die there, on the island. Could be he's right."

Ahead of them, Griffin stopped. He'd come to a small

wooden door. "Father never told me about this. I found it, but I never told. You see, he could've trusted me, but he never gave me the chance. He could've trusted me."

Well, Twig didn't trust him—though, knowing what it was like not to be trusted, she felt a pang of guilt for it. Twig mustered a smile for Griffin. "Thank you," she said. Ben wouldn't say it, but someone should, just in case. Just in case he wasn't who Ben thought he was. Just in case, even if Griffin was who Ben thought he was right now, he could ever be somebody different.

Griffin bent down and lifted a blanket from a small pile next to the door, revealing Ben and Twig's bows and quivers, their swords, and Ben's dagger. A new belt for Ben, to replace the one he'd cut, and his jacket and cloak.

Griffin held Twig's weapons out. "It wasn't easy getting these back. I thought about taking some from the armory instead, but I knew you'd rather have your own."

"Thank you."

Griffin glanced at her swollen hand and looked worried. Ben quickly donned his weapons, as though they might be snatched away any moment.

Griffin opened the door, revealing yet another flight of stairs. But it was short, and when Twig shone her flashlight on it, she could see that another wooden door was above it, where the ceiling of the passage ought to be. Griffin ascended the steps and reached over his head and eased the creaking door open. The fresh night air rushed down at Twig. She breathed deep and stepped up before Ben.

When she reached the top, her head emerged just above the forest floor. The door to the tunnel lay on the ground outside. She planted her hands on the leaf-strewn earth and cried out in pain, then scrambled awkwardly out with Ben boosting her from behind and Griffin pulling on her good hand.

Griffin gave Ben directions to an abandoned woods-man's cottage, where he said they would find everything they needed—including Wonder and Rain Cloud. Griffin claimed he'd sent word to Merrill as to what had happened through Pete, and that Merrill would be waiting for them at his place.

Silverforest was not as dark as the forest of Lonehorn Island, but still, it was dark, and so vast. Ben had never been through this door. How did he even know exactly where they were?

"Griffin," Twig said, intentionally avoiding Ben's gaze. "Can't you take us there?"

He shook his head. "I have to get back before I'm missed."

Ben grabbed Twig's sleeve. He turned and started on his way at a jog. Twig hurried to keep up. There would be only one thing on Ben's mind now—finding Indy.

•••

Ben opened the battered oak door of the cottage a crack. He shouldered his bow and drew his sword, even as he joined Twig in talking encouragingly to the animals inside. There was no mistaking Rain Cloud's snort or Wonder's wild whinny, but he couldn't be sure of anything Griffin was involved in.

"Ben, hurry up!" Twig said.

"Stand back," he warned her. "She's been waiting a long time to see you too. What if she comes rushing out?"

Twig stepped back. He stuck the toe of his boot in the crack and eased the door open. Twig leaned around Ben and shone her flashlight into the shadowy damps beyond the doorway. A sharp white horn cut through the darkness above the flashlight beam.

Wonder leaped circles around them. As Twig laughed and calmed her, Ben struggled to stay calm himself. He took Rain Cloud's head in his hands and gave him a good rub behind the ears. Soon he'd have his unicorn back too. They'd gotten out of that dungeon. Not how he'd expected, but they'd gotten out. Now he could find Indy—and send word to Reynald that their duel was still on. They would find a way to conduct their challenge without the queen stopping them.

Chapter 23

THE SAFE HOUSE MERRILL had been staying in was an isolated little stone construction barely a step up from the herder's outpost. At first Twig feared it was empty, but Merrill appeared, hurrying across the little yard to greet them, a lantern shrouded with cloth in his hand. From the silvery leaves overhead came a familiar coo. Emmie glided onto Ben's shoulder.

Merrill motioned to the outbuilding that passed for a stable. Ben dismounted, and Merrill said, "I'm sorry, Ben-boy. I'd hoped that if you got a chance to talk to her—"

"I know."

"I was tempted to try to meet you partway, but I knew you wouldn't be fool enough to take the road, and I feared we'd pass each other right by. I'm glad my directions got to you all right."

"They got to me through Griffin. That's not all right, Merrill. This house isn't safe anymore, and you know it."

"I'll find another place for Marble soon enough."

Merrill gave Wonder a quick greeting and proffered an

acorn from his pocket. Wonder accepted the toll and let Merrill pass to Twig's side. He raised his hands to her. "Come on now, Twig-girl, before you fall off."

Merrill's arms were so strong and welcoming, his eyes so earnest and kind, Twig realized just how tired she was and how scared, and how tired of just being scared, and she slid into his grasp.

Ben dismounted on his own, though Merrill watched his every move with concern.

"You hurt, Ben-boy?"

"No, we're fine, apart from being worn out."

"Here." Merrill handed Twig off to Ben. "You get this one inside and rest. And eat something, the both of you, before you faint." Merrill took hold of Wonder's bridle. "I'll get the animals settled."

Inside the house, there was a good, warm fire and a pot of something that smelled wonderful—almost as good as Mrs. Murley's pot roast—simmering over some embers. Near the hearth, a small, knee-high table was set with three spoons, three mugs, and three napkins. A pitcher of milk and a metal trivet coated with chipped white enamel sat in the middle of the table. The trivet was circular in shape, and the negative space in its center formed a unicorn, forelegs raised, horn held high. It looked like it was dancing right in front of a full moon.

Ben said, "Go on. Sit down."

Twig eyed the cushions, trying to figure out which one was Merrill's.

"Just sit, Twig. It's not the queen's table."

"I know that."

Ben knelt beside her and poured milk into the mug in front of her, then into one of the other mugs. Twig gulped it greedily. Ben found a thick, folded-up cloth and used it to carefully pick up the bubbling pot and lug it to the table. It was a big, black, iron thing. When Ben removed the lid, Twig nearly cried with gratitude. It looked so good and so hot, and she was so hungry. If Merrill hadn't ordered them to go ahead and eat without him, she would've gladly cast aside any concerns about manners that the Murleys had worked so hard to instill in her.

She grabbed her spoon and sat up on her knees and aimed the utensil at the contents of the pot, but her hand collided with Ben's. He laughed with a crooked, tired smile. Anxious as he was to find Indy, she could see the fatigue overcoming Ben. He'd have gone straight to the swamp from the castle, but he didn't want Griffin to know they were headed there, and their chances of success in the swamp were much better in the daylight.

"I was going to serve some up for you." He retreated with his spoon and sat back on his heels. "But go ahead."

She would, thank you very much. It was beef stew or something like it. She didn't bother to ask Ben what it was; she just filled her bowl and sat back and scooped up a bite.

"It's hot," Ben warned as he filled his own bowl.

Twig gave the spoonful a perfunctory blow, then sucked a bit of the broth. Hot, hot! But so good.

The stew was cool enough for Twig to shovel up heaping bites by the time Merrill came in, knocking the crud off his boots at the doorstep.

"Any good?" Merrill said.

Twig's mouth was so full she would have sprayed Ben with broth had she tried to open it. She nodded vigorously.

Ben said, "Better than I even remembered."

Merrill sat down with them, and Ben filled his mug and his bowl for him.

"Thank you, Ben-boy."

They all ate in silence for a while, then Merrill said, "So? What's this about the Boy King? And our Indy?"

Ben began to tell Merrill their story. Twig considered her empty bowl and whether it would be appropriate to fill it a third time. Why not? She helped herself while Ben and Merrill talked.

That night, Merrill dug a bunch of blankets out of a big wooden trunk, dragged the table aside, and laid them on the hearth for Twig and Ben. They settled there with the warmth of the glowing embers in the fireplace at their heads and the draft from the cracks around the doorway at their feet.

CHAPTER 24

BEN COULDN'T SLEEP ANY longer. He eyed the crack under the door. It would be light enough soon. He stepped over Merrill's sleeping form, grabbed his weapons—just in case—and eased the door open. Sword in hand, he headed for the stable to take care of Wonder and Rain Cloud and get them ready for their journey to the Death Swamp.

Ben didn't take more than two steps before the dim early morning light revealed something strange. A large, mud-spattered white form curled on the ground right in front of the stable. Ben hurried closer. A deep snuffle came from the unicorn. Its head was tucked against powerful forelegs, extended horn resting on the ground. A dark blue stripe spiraled around it.

"Indy!" Ben threw down his sword and almost flung his arm around his stallion's neck. But that was no way to wake a sleeping unicorn, not if he wanted to make it through another day.

"Indy-boy." Ben waited for Indy's ears to prick, his head to lift, him to nicker a morning greeting. To nuzzle him and listen to him ask where he'd been. Indy nickered, but it was just another muffled dream sound. Ben dared to put a hand on Indy's flank. "Morning, boy. I missed you so much. Come on, are you not going to say hello?"

Indy snored loudly. Something was wrong. Just like that morning on the island when he wouldn't wake up.

"Twig! Merrill!" he called. "It's Indy!"

Twig skidded out of the house, donning her weapons.

Ben grabbed her arm and steadied her. "He's here. Indy's here."

"What? How?"

"I don't know, but he won't wake up."

"Like before?"

Merrill emerged in the yard. "What's all this now?"

"Indy's back, but…"

Merrill knelt next to the unicorn. "Something's not right, I think."

Ben nodded. He studied the trees surrounding the clearing. Had someone brought Indy here or had Indy found them on his own? Could someone have followed him and Twig last night? Were they still there, watching? "Twig, you'd better check on Wonder."

"You two stay here," Merrill said. "I'd better have a look around."

Ben stood next to Indy, bow ready, as Merrill disappeared into the trees.

Moments later, Twig emerged from the stable. "Wonder

and Marble are asleep too, even with all this fuss—but not Rain Cloud or Franklin or the cow." Twig tried to smile. "Don't worry. They came around last time. The important thing is that Indy's back."

Something snapped in the trees from the opposite direction Merrill had gone. The subtlest of sounds, but—someone was there, Ben knew it. In a blink, he had an arrow nocked. Bowstring taut, he took a step forward, toward the sound.

"What is it?" Twig whispered as she readied her bow.

"I thought I heard something."

Snap.

This time the sound was behind them. Ben turned and looked right into Indy's wakeful quicksilver eyes.

"They're awake!" Twig cried, abandoning her bow. "That must've been what you heard." She ran into the stable, where Wonder was nickering.

Indy's voice, fully awake, calling out to Ben, brought the undercurrent of emotions to the surface. "Where have you been, Indy-boy?" Ben shouldered his bow and buried his face in Indy's mane, hiding tears of relief.

Wonder bounced outside, then danced up a storm and darted to her father's side. Ben reluctantly backed away and stood next to Twig to watch their reunion.

Rain Cloud emerged, shaking his head at the braying donkey. Twig hugged Rain Cloud, and the pony gave the unicorns a smug look. They might have each other, but he had Twig all to himself. Feeling left out, Ben gave Rain Cloud a rub under the chin.

"We got Indy back," Twig said. "Now we can go home."

And then what? The thief had shown them he could get through the passage and take Ben's unicorn while he slept. Maybe Mr. Murley was right. Ben should move in. They could add a stall for Indy too. He wouldn't like it, but it was better than being stolen and dragged into Terracornus, wasn't it? In time, maybe he'd get used to it.

Except that Indy hadn't been dragged. There was no evidence of that.

"I don't get it," Twig said. "If this thief, or whoever it was, put them all to sleep somehow, if he put Indy to sleep in the hollow, how'd he get him through the passage? How'd he get him anywhere? Unless—"

"Unless?"

"He hypnotized them. I saw a guy do it in a show at the fair."

"The fair?"

"It's a thing they have every year in Puyallup. There are rides and shows and lots of food...never mind. It doesn't matter. The hypnotist looked the people in the eyes, and he talked to them and moved his finger. They followed his finger with their eyes, and before you knew it, they were in a kind of trance. It was sort of like a magic show."

"I told you, there's no such thing as magic."

"It's not magic. It's just one of those things that no one can really explain. A sort of trick. He could make the people do all kinds of silly things. Walk around and cluck like chickens. Afterward, he brought them back. They were themselves again."

"If the unicorn thief did something like that...how did Indy and Wonder wake up?" Ben peered into the trees. He was out there somewhere, he knew it. And so was Merrill. Ben's heart pounded. He readied his bow again.

Twig shifted her feet uneasily. "Maybe it just wears off eventually. Maybe that night, in the hollow, the thief was testing it out on Indy and Wonder to see if it worked on them."

"But why just put them to sleep? Why not make them follow him if that's what he does?"

"Maybe he wasn't expecting two unicorns, and one of them made a noise and woke us up before he could finish, so he just put them to sleep so we couldn't come after him." Twig's eyes got bigger. "Do you think he was going to take both of them? Do you think he would've, if Wonder was there when he came again?"

"I don't know. He would have needed Wonder under his spell either way, in order to take off with Indy. But, Twig, how could he sneak up on them like that?"

"Merrill said he was good."

Ben hugged Indy, resting the side of his face against his velvety neck. "What did he want with you, Indy-boy? Why did he just give you back?"

Twig smiled proudly. "Maybe Indy was more than he could handle, even with his hypnotic spell powers. He got away and almost got lost in the Death Swamp after all."

"If that's what happened, the thief was able to find him and recapture him." He was good. Who knew what else he was good at?

Ben whistled for Merrill. To his great relief, his old friend whistled back. The brush parted, and Merrill stepped back into the clearing. "He was out there, I think, but he's gone now. I'm afraid I won't be much good tracking him on foot." Merrill patted his artificial leg. "Too noisy."

"Let's just get them fed and get them home," Twig said.

Merrill nodded at the animals. "They're not the only ones who need to be fed," Merrill said. "If you two can take care of the animals, I'll go back in and get some breakfast going."

•••

Merrill served them something that resembled oatmeal for breakfast. There was a pot of honey in the middle of the table. Twig made good use of it, coating her food in honey, then drenching it with the especially creamy milk Merrill kept on hand. Straight from the poor, pestered cow. It was a wonder the cow's milk hadn't gone sour after a night with a grumpy pony and a restless, half-wild creature.

Twig jumped. Wonder and Indy whickered warnings from the stable. Marble joined in. Twig knew that sound. *Another unicorn is coming.*

They rushed outside just in time to see a unicorn gallop onto the property.

Ben was ready to shoot when Merrill said, "It's all right, Ben-boy."

The unicorn's rider dismounted. "So, you made it," the rider said.

Griffin!

Ben shouldered his bow. "You again?"

"What's the matter? You thought you'd get away with never seeing me again? I had to make my appearance at the castle and give Mother the news that you'd escaped. I promised to find you and to bring you back."

"Are you in the habit of making promises you cannot keep?" Ben's hand moved within easy draw of his sword. "Or did you let me go just so you could be the one who captured me?"

"I let you go so I could help you and then bring you back, and that's exactly what's going to happen. I'm going to help you take your friend to the passage, and then I'm going to bring you home to Mother. Merrill agreed to help."

"Merrill?"

"I had to tell him, Ben. And let him have his say. It was Griffin who sent me word of how things went with your mother. Griffin who told Pete and arranged to get you out. Agreeing to his terms was the only way I could get Twig back home."

Ben turned from Merrill to his brother. "I'm *not* coming back, except to face Reynald in that duel!"

"Then there's nothing I can do for you but take you back now." Griffin's hands clenched at his sides. His face got redder, and his knuckles got whiter. "I won't let you die in that swamp or on that cursed island."

Ben's fingers wrapped around his sword hilt. Twig put the palm of her good hand on his chest, holding him back before he could draw it. She gave him what she hoped was a calming look, but when she stepped between the brothers and looked up at Griffin, she felt the tears of anger and hopelessness sting her eyes.

She didn't allow herself to look away. "It's not a cursed island! It's our home, and the herd needs us. We're going to make things right there, and we're going to settle this thing with Eastland whether that means we die doing it or not!" The tears streamed down Twig's cheeks. Her heart pounded, making her injured left hand throb with a pain of even greater intensity.

Griffin stood there, looking stunned. "Merrill?"

Merrill shook his head. "I've met my part of your bargain, Griffin. I'm not fool enough to try to make Ben do anything he doesn't want to do. You cannot blame him for not wanting to go back there, I think. Not after what happened."

Griffin looked deflated for a moment. Then an angry determination, not so unlike what Twig had seen several times in Ben, took over. Twig thought he might actually try to take Ben by force. But then, without another word, he mounted his unicorn and rode away, into the silvery-dawn shadows of the forest. Twig had a feeling it wasn't over. Griffin wouldn't give up. And Ben was wrong about his brother wanting to get rid of him. He'd find another way to try to keep Ben in Terracornus.

CHAPTER 25

SO MANY TIMES BEN had sat around the Murleys' table and felt strangely thrilled—and sometimes overwhelmed—by the chattering of all the girls, their endless questions. Today, the dinner table was uncomfortably quiet. The Murleys' disappointment seemed to have dampened even Twig's appetite. Mr. Murley said the prayer this time, thanking God for bringing all the girls home safely several days ago, and now, bringing Twig and Ben, the unicorns, and Rain Cloud too. He asked for wisdom to know what to do about this situation. *Which situation?* Ben couldn't help wondering. All of them defying the rules and sneaking out, or the fact that the passage had been compromised?

Twig had let Ben do most of the explaining. She hadn't said a word when he failed to mention their visit to the queen. Or the dungeon. Or their scrape with the Boy King. Or the duel.

When they'd asked about her hand, Twig had simply said, "It got stepped on."

The Murleys knew little more than that they'd gone to Terracornus, found Indy, and brought him back.

After helping clear the table, Ben slipped away to be with Indy in the pasture. He needed to think, and Twig needed to smooth things over with her foster parents.

•••

Something pattered against the window. Twig looked up from her schoolwork and saw a bright green blur of wings.

"It's Emmie!" Taylor exclaimed.

"She's looking for Ben," Regina said. "Just leave her alone. She'll find him."

That was true, but if Emmie had a message, Twig wanted to get to it first. She'd had enough of Ben's secrecy. She pushed back the little burning feeling that it was wrong, and she followed Casey and Taylor as they ran to the front door.

"She's so pretty," Taylor said. "I want to see if she'll come to me."

Casey threw open the door. Emmie was already headed for the pasture. A swath of white stood out against the shadows of the pasture shelter. There was Ben, deep in conversation with Indy while Wonder pranced in the rain.

"Emmie," Taylor cooed. Emmie cooed back and landed on Taylor's extended arm.

"Look! There's a note," Casey said. "Maybe it's from Merrill. When are we gonna get to meet Merrill, anyway?"

There was a brief note in Merrill's handwriting, a smaller piece of paper rolled around the outside of a larger, more substantial one—sealed with gold wax and stamped with a fancy letter *R*. Around the *R*, Twig made out the word *Eastland*. Merrill's note confirmed that he had forwarded it to Ben from the Boy King. With a burst of defiance, Twig popped the seal and opened Reynald's letter.

Casey peered over her arm. "The dwooo…?"

"Duel," Twig whispered numbly.

"Duel!" Casey gasped.

"Give me that!" Regina said.

Twig held the note away, but it was too late. Regina had seen it.

Regina eyed her questioningly. "The duel is on?"

"Duel?" Janessa said. "Like in Casey's stories?"

"Shh!" all the girls said together.

"Too late." In the doorway, Mrs. Murley held out her hand, and Twig reluctantly gave her the note. She glanced at Twig as she read.

Ben noticed the commotion and came running up the front walk. Emmie fluttered to Ben. He held his arm out for her and blinked at the note in Mrs. Murley's hand.

"This is for you, Ben." She passed him the message.

Emmie hopped to his shoulder. Something glimmered in Ben's eyes—something that looked astonishingly like happiness. At the thought of a duel? Twig wanted to shake him. She'd spent the last couple of days regretting her bold words to Griffin and trying to convince Ben to come up with a way to fix things without getting himself killed.

When Ben finished reading, he looked from the broken seal to Twig, his expression clouded with accusation. Until he saw Mrs. Murley's face, set in determination against his crazy schemes.

"What does this mean?"

"Oh. This…" He twisted a fold of his cape in his hand.

"Well? 'The duel is on. We will meet on our sides of the Death Swamp on the sixth day of the month of Silver Breeze.'"

Ben counted silently on his fingers. "That's June first."

"Not the date. The *duel*, Ben."

Ben didn't answer Mrs. Murley. Twig bit her lip, trying to decide whether she should do it for him.

"Here in the Earth Land," Mrs. Murley said, "a duel is when two people face off against each other to settle a dispute. Often the loser ends up seriously wounded, even dead. What does it mean in Terracornus?"

"The same, mostly."

"No one's going to die!" Twig said. "No people and no unicorns either."

"But I have to do it! You agreed!"

"Yes, you have to do it. But we have to find a way for you to win without killing Reynald."

"Reynald!" Janessa said, no doubt recalling the stories Ben had told them.

"The Boy King," said Casey. "He's fierce and swift, and his stallion, Stone Heart, never wavers."

All eyes turned on Ben.

Ben struggled to smile. "She sure likes stories. I didn't know about the duel when I told her. Besides, it's not as bad as that. She just tells it better."

Mrs. Murley said, "There are better ways to settle differences than a duel."

Ben's jaw twitched like he wanted to say something. Something he was afraid would come out disrespectful.

Before Twig could figure out what to say herself, Casey said, "Not for Reynald the Boy King. He's impossible. The only one worse is the queen. She—"

"Shh!" all the girls said again.

Casey blinked back tears, and Twig slipped an arm around her shoulders and gave her a pat with her bandaged hand. She wanted to glare at Ben for filling Casey's head so full of stories about Terracornus that they kept leaking out. But that wouldn't do, not when they had to convince Mrs. Murley he had his head on straight.

• • •

In moments they were all back in the living room, piled on the couches and spilling onto the rug. Mr. Murley leaned forward in the recliner and called the meeting to order.

"Girls," he said calmly, firmly.

The chattering and squirming and pulling out of cushions from underneath each other stopped instantly. Amazing, how he did that. Ben made a note to himself to figure out how it was done.

"So, Ben, let's hear about this Death Swamp Duel."

"It's a way for two riders to settle a dispute without their whole divisions—or now, their entire lands—going to war."

Mr. Murley raised an eyebrow. "So duels save lives."

"Tell him about the Death Swamp," Casey hissed. "Just the smell of the Death Swamp makes the bravest riders shake in their boots. The water's so stinkified—so foul—it breathes fire."

"Fire-breathing water?"

Mrs. Murley's eyes begged Ben to deny it, but he couldn't. It was true. "The duel used to be fought down in the mud. In the swamp itself. But so many duelers died without even settling their disputes, that a boardwalk was built through the swamp. There are some narrower boardwalks that you can enter from the north and south sides of the swamp to get to the main boardwalk, but those aren't used for duels."

"So the fire-breathing water is avoided completely," Twig said.

"But if you falled, the gators would eat you."

"Casey!"

"She's right. Animals can smell blood, you know," Regina said.

"There are alligators?" Mr. Murley asked.

"Swamp lizards," all the girls said together.

"They're like alligators," Casey explained.

Ben sat back and crossed his arms. "I won't fall."

"But one of you has to fall. Isn't that how it works?" Mr. Murley pressed him.

"The flag of each rider is planted on one end of the swamp. Each rider starts on the end of the swamp where his flag is. A rider has to go through the swamp, take his opponent's flag, and come out of the swamp with it in order to win."

"But one of them usually dies," Regina said.

Casey nodded, giving Ben a defiant look.

"What about Stone Heart?" Mandy said in a hushed voice.

Casey nodded. "The Boy King's unicorn. He's never met his match."

Ben squared his shoulders and looked into each girl's eyes. "Stone Heart never met Indigo Independence!"

A gathering of herdsmen would've raised fists and voices in a cheer at that. The girls hugged each other tighter. Mr. and Mrs. Murley exchanged silent looks.

Ben was still trying to make out what Twig thought, whose

side she was going to take, when she spoke up. "I'm going to figure something out. There's going to be a duel to save Westland and Eastland from going to war. Ben's going to win for Westland, but he's going to do it without getting killed—and without killing the Boy King, Reynald."

The girls murmured. Casey looked at Twig doubtfully.

Twig's shoulders sagged. She too had hoped for cheers. A crazy thing to hope for, since what she'd just proposed was even more unlikely than Ben's claim that he could win.

"Twig," Mr. Murley said, "Ben, girls, I think Mrs. Murley and I are going to discuss this on our own now."

"Yes," Mrs. Murley said. "Back to work, all of you."

Back to work is right. Whatever the Murleys said, he had a duel to win in six weeks. He had to prepare—for the fight and for the fact that these might be his last days with Indy. The end of his dreams, of his father's dreams for him. Would his father really want him to do this? He'd entrusted him with the island and its herd. That's what he'd want him to focus on, not Terracornus and all its problems. Problems he'd warned Ben could destroy him. He didn't care what Merrill said; Ben was certain his father would've never wanted Ben to go back there and get involved. But the unicorn thief had given him no choice.

That's not true. I made a choice at the banquet. A decision all my own.

CHAPTER 26

BEN WHISPERED ONE LAST apology to Indy, gave Wonder a pat, and closed the door to their stall. Twig stood in the aisle waiting for him. Five more faces peered eagerly around her. The girls of Island Ranch had called a secret meeting to discuss the duel during evening chore time.

Normally, one or both of the Murleys would be out in the stable helping to get the animals ready for the night, but tonight they were in the house, huddled over cups of coffee, having a meeting of their own. About how to keep Ben from the duel, no doubt. Maybe even about how to keep either of them from going back to Terracornus. Ben had warned Twig this gathering with the girls had better not turn into the same kind of meeting.

"Did you bring it?" Casey's big brown eyes brimmed with hope and anticipation.

Ben pulled out the rolled-up map. He'd told Twig that sharing the map with the girls was a bad idea, but she'd insisted they needed as much information as they could get in order to come up with a plan.

Twig was stubborn. There was no point in trying to argue with her. But she was smart too. She'd see soon enough that he was right. There was no easy way—no safe way—to win a Death Swamp Duel.

The cluster of girls spread out around the edges of the stable aisle. Ponies nickered curiously from their stalls. Twig brushed stray wood shavings from the dirt floor, and Ben knelt and rolled out the map. Twilight glowed through the skylights overhead, a springlike, jewel blue, while mist drifted past the stable windows, making its brightness, its hope, feel even farther away, even more out of reach.

The map of the Death Swamp spoke of a much grimmer reality. Ben's reality. Everything that stood between him and his hopes. His very future. Maybe his dying for the unicorns of Westland would remind his mother and Griffin what was really important.

The girls got down on knees and bellies. They held down the curling paper with elbows and palms.

"Ooh!" Janessa said.

"Cree-py," Mandy said under breath.

Heavy black letters labeled the map: *Death Swamp, Duels and Disasters*. The unfortunate words were too big to try to hide them from the girls.

Ben said, "The man who made this map was very…interested in the swamp and its stories."

"You mean obsessed!" Regina said. "Look at all those drawings!"

Along the border of the map, swamp lizards snapped their powerful jaws, full of crooked, blackened teeth. Serpents slithered around the swords and toxic gasses swirled among the bows of fallen travelers and duelers, reminding the viewer that weapons couldn't save anyone unwise enough to wander into the wrong part of the swamp from their deadly poison.

"It's beautifully drawn." Twig's eyes moved hungrily over the ink renderings accented with watercolor. Her finger hovered over lines, and he could see her contemplating how they were made, how she might do the same. Finally, she looked up at Ben. "Is it old?"

Ben smoothed out a wrinkle over the signature: *Elijah Murley*. "A family heirloom."

Casey mouthed *Murley*, making little whispering sounds, as she couldn't help doing whenever she read to herself. She looked up at Ben. "We'll be careful," she promised solemnly.

"Move your feet," Mandy muttered to Regina. "They're dirty."

Regina gave Mandy a little slap on the arm, but she pulled her feet back.

Taylor scrunched up her forehead in thought. "Is it still current, though?"

Ben smiled. "Nothing much changes in the Death Swamp.

Here you can see the entrance to the boardwalk on the Eastland side. And here it is on the Westland side."

"Look at that!" Taylor braced herself against Janessa's knee and leaned forward, trying not to touch the map.

In the south end of the swamp, a blue flame burst from the water. Thankfully, Elijah had enough of the Earth Land's sense of propriety not to include the body of the swamp fire's victim. Instead, there was a simple cross labeled *John of Redbud*, along with the date of his unfortunate death. Here and there, a pure white horn protruded from swamp grass or mud, and the name of a brave and beloved mount was penned.

Casey touched her fingertip to the image of swamp fire, then pulled back, cringing as though it had singed her. "It's like a great big story," she whispered. "A great big, scary story."

Beside him, Ben felt Twig tense. Then she straightened up. "Yes, it looks scary. And that's why we're here, to try to find a way to help Ben through it."

Casey said, "I know. We could train Emmie to grab the Boy King's flag. Ben wouldn't even have to go into the swamp. She could just fly to the other side, high enough the fire can't get her and—"

"That would be cheating," Mandy said.

Casey looked to Ben.

"The contestant has to take the flag," he said. "No one else can do it for him."

Her face fell. "Not even a bird?"

Twig shook her head and gave Casey a squeeze. "It was a good idea, though."

Taylor cupped her chin in her palm, leaning on her elbows. "What exactly are the rules?"

"We have to go through the swamp and—"

"Through the swamp!" Twig cried. "So, you don't *have* to use the boardwalk! Look. The boardwalk weaves through the swamp." She traced her finger over the snakelike line. "It's not the fastest route."

Ben crossed his arms. "It's the only route."

"But what if it isn't?"

"Twig, they didn't build that boardwalk for nothing. You cannot get through the swamp without it."

"How did they build it, then?"

"They had men keeping watch all around them, shooting the swamp lizards whenever they came close."

"Couldn't *you* shoot the swamp lizards?"

"Could be I could shoot *a* swamp lizard, but *every* swamp lizard, before it has a chance to attack? I don't have a crew to keep watch. Besides, the boardwalk is built like this," he said, making the snaking motion with his arm, "because it follows the easiest route through the swamp. If we tried to brave the mud, it would have to be right alongside the boardwalk. Otherwise Indy and I would be waist deep—or worse—in water. Water full of swamp lizards."

Regina pushed her thick, dark hair back. "There wouldn't be much point in avoiding the boardwalk if you had to travel right next to it. You'd still end up fighting, only you'd be fighting in the mud."

"Twig, you brought the computer, right?"

Twig nodded at Taylor, unzipped her shell, and turned the mini-backpack she always wore under her jacket toward Taylor. Taylor took out the slim little tablet computer the Murleys had recently gotten for the girls to share. That contraption had Ben second-guessing whether there was such a thing as magic. Pictures broken into tiny, invisible bits and floating through the air, reassembled on the glowing screen—a screen that changed every time he touched it.

"What are you doing?" he asked.

"Research," Twig answered for Taylor. "Search for ways to get through a swamp."

"Swamp safety!" Janessa chimed in.

"Swamp monsters!" said Casey.

"But this is the Death Swamp!" Ben said. "Unless you have death swamps in the Earth Land—"

"We have swamps," Mandy said.

"And swamp men," Casey added.

"Those aren't real."

"How do you know?"

Twig gave Casey a look, and she and Mandy shut their

mouths and sat back. "I know it's not the same," Twig told Ben, "but we have to figure this out."

"There's nothing to figure out. If you want to help me, then help me practice." Ben reached for the map, to roll it back up. If Twig wasn't going to help him get ready, then maybe he should get out of this place before the Murleys did anything to try to stop him.

"Got it!" Taylor grinned over the tablet. "A pirogue!"

Ben let go of the map and looked at the glowing screen Taylor held up. "A what?"

"It's a boat made specially for using in swamps. Look. It has a flat bottom. Wonder and Indy could stand in it. And they're light and easy to carry."

Regina scrolled down the screen. "Yeah, but they're found mostly in the South. Louisiana, Florida…where are we going to get a pirogue in Washington state?"

Taylor frowned, then tapped and scrolled with renewed determination. "There!" She turned the computer around so they all could see.

"'Pirogue kits. Easy to build pirogues for beginners. Two-day delivery available.' We could have it shipped to Cedar Harbor and take *Blue Molly* to pick it up."

"*Blue Molly?*"

"The Murleys' boat," Twig explained.

Janessa looked over Taylor's shoulder. "They list all the

supplies you need, and they send the hard parts, like the ribs, already made!"

Ben took the tablet and read the list. He turned to Twig. "What's plywood?"

"It's like fake wood." Mandy made a face.

"It's not fake. It's pressed together," Twig corrected.

"The point," Taylor said, "is that it's light and inexpensive."

Twig studied the series of pictures on the website, showing the steps involved in building the pirogue. "We just might be able to do this."

"Mr. M could help us build it," Janessa said. "If we explain that you'll be safe in the boat—"

"Wait a minute," Ben said. "I won't be safe in a boat in the Death Swamp. This pirogue, it's not a bad idea, but..." He glanced nervously at Twig. "No one's tried to boat through that water in hundreds of years—if ever. And if I do make it through, I've left Westland's flag completely unprotected during the trip. If Reynald gets there first, I won't be there to stop him. I won't even know. He'll just ride right down the boardwalk and take my flag without even a fight."

"That's what we're trying to do. Not fight, right?" Casey said.

"If I'm just going to let him take Westland's flag, I might as well not even show up!"

"You won't have to worry about the flag, because he won't get there first." Twig put her hands on the map, one on each side of the Death Swamp. "Look how narrow the swamp is, compared to the length of the boardwalk."

"But a pirogue just floats along," Regina said. "It's slow. If the Boy King is galloping along—"

Ben straightened up. He set the computer aside. "He cannot gallop."

"What?"

"The boardwalk is rickety. It's old. It cannot take pounding hooves. Parts of it are even sagging into the swamp and have to be jumped. A rider has to go slowly, cautiously."

"So it *could* work!" Twig said.

Janessa's mouth sagged in a rare frown. "Isn't it kinda cheating though?"

Twig shrugged. "It's not against the rules. Ben, you could do this."

"*If* I didn't have to worry about the dangers of the swamp, yes, a boat could get to the other side faster, I think. But—"

"You have a map. A good one. You know where the swamp fire is and where the swamp lizards nest. And if you can shoot from the back of a unicorn, you can do it standing in a boat."

"Twig—"

"It's the only way, Ben. You'll have us all behind you. Otherwise…"

"I'll think about it." Ben waved the girls off the map and rolled it up. He had no intention of doing any such thing.

"He's mad," Casey whispered.

Of course he was mad. Twig was supposed to be his partner. Hadn't she said so when he'd tried to go looking for Indy by himself? And now she was siding with all of them, against him.

They are her family. The thought cut him. Hadn't he told her that? But where did that leave him? Alone, that's where. No one in his family would side with him. Probably Merrill wouldn't either. Especially if Twig convinced him not to.

Twig whispered something to Taylor and Casey, and they grabbed the other girls by the hand and left the stable.

Good riddance.

"You can do this, Ben." Twig's eyes gleamed with determination.

"You want to build a pirogue," Ben said as he tucked the map away. "Here, at the ranch?"

"Well, we'd need Mr. Murley's help with the supplies and the tools."

Ben strode to the tack room and began to gather Indy's things. "It's not going to happen. Mr. Murley won't do it."

"Ben! What are you doing?"

"Going back to Terracornus."

"You can't!"

"I cannot let this war happen either—not when I know there's a thing I can do about it. The unicorns' numbers are dwindling. If Eastland and Westland break their truce, others will be drawn into the war with them. It's not just that so many unicorns will die—this could lead to them dying out altogether."

"You can't go. What if they take Indy? Besides, you can't do this all by yourself."

"I would've been able to do it if I'd *kept* it to myself. Now they all know, and what am I supposed to do?"

Twig opened her mouth to argue, then sank deeper into her shell. Into her old self.

Much as it pained Ben to see it, he couldn't resist going on. "You took that message. That message that was supposed to be for me, and now they all know, and the Murleys are going to try to stop me!"

Teary blue eyes regarded him above the quivering collar of Twig's shell. She turned to leave. But then she poked her chin out and wiped her eyes. "I'm sorry, Ben. I messed up."

Ben looked away so he wouldn't have to watch her tears. She made a little choking sound.

Then her voice steadied and she said, "But you're about to mess things up even worse if you leave. You're going to get killed—if you don't get captured again. You're so worried about the Murleys, but what do you think your mother will do?"

"She isn't going to know. Not until it's over."

"If you don't want her to find out, then you have to stay

here. No one here can tell her what you're getting ready to do. No one even knows how. And don't forget about the unicorn thief! He knew where you were. What if he still knows? You know Indy's safer here in the stable than he is out there in Silverforest."

"I have to do what I have to do, Twig."

"Just give me two more days. Two more days to convince the Murleys."

She was so sure. So sure she could fix everything. That was probably his fault more than anyone's. So Ben said, "Fine. Two days," and he wondered what Twig was going to do when she figured out she was wrong.

CHAPTER 27

THE SPRING SUN PEEKED through the treetops, drying the long nets of lichen that hung from the cedars and shook with the breeze. But back at the ranch, Twig had seen dark clouds moving toward the island. Soon the rain would come.

After a big Saturday breakfast, she'd proposed the plan to boat through the Death Swamp to the Murleys, and they'd said they would have to discuss it. So she and Ben had headed into the woods to check on Bounce and to bring the injured unicorn a blanket—hopefully before it started to rain.

They found Bounce in the same spot, though this time she'd heard their approach and was on her feet. She stepped tentatively out of her little nest in the ferns to say hello.

"She's walking!" Twig whispered, though she wanted to shout.

"She's a little wobbly, but she's definitely looking better."

Ben dismounted and told Indy to stay. Twig stayed astride Wonder, unsure whether she could trust her not to spook

Bounce just yet. A drop of rain fell on Twig's cheek, then another on her shoulder. Just a few sprinkles so far.

Ben held his hand out and, under Indy's watchful eye, Bounce lipped his fingers. They fed her and watered her, but when they went to leave, the unicorn limped after them. Her nicker verged on a whimper. *Take me with you, please. Don't leave me here all by myself.*

The rain began to fall in earnest. Twig lingered, looking into the pools of Bounce's lonely eyes. "Do you think she could make it back to the ranch?"

"Back to the ranch?"

"She's helpless and alone. She could stay there, just until she gets better. What if one of her herd mates turns on her? What if the thief comes back?"

"I don't think a thief would take an unhealthy unicorn."

"Maybe her being sick will make her an easier target. One he can't resist. He took Indy when he was the only unicorn. Maybe he hasn't taken any of the others because they're not alone."

Ben sighed deeply. He turned his face up to the trees.

"I know," Twig said. "This isn't how it's supposed to work. You're supposed to be out here—we're supposed to be out here—and the herd is supposed to stay wild. But we have to protect her."

"All right. Let's see if she wants to come."

• • •

From Bedtime Story's stall, Rain Cloud snorted his discontent. Story, Casey's good-natured pony, nickered an attempt to cheer him up. She seemed glad for the company. But she hadn't had to give up her stall to a strange unicorn, as Rain Cloud had. Ben watched Twig scratch his forehead and kiss his snout.

"It's only for a little while," she said tenderly.

How did Twig do it—torn between Rain Cloud and Wonder, the ranch and the wild whispers of the island, here and her other home, with her father and stepmother? He hadn't given nearly enough thought to it before he met the Murleys.

Bounce whined nervously, and Mr. Murley stroked her neck as he eyed the wound on her side. Bounce wouldn't let Mrs. Murley or any of the other girls come close, but she warmed to Mr. Murley right away.

"What a lovely mare you are, Bounce." Mr. Murley turned to Ben. "It's hard to think she has a vicious side. Strange, isn't it, what a creature can be capable of? Violence one day, gentleness the next…"

A memory rushed back at Ben like a splash of scalding water. His mother smiling, dusting him off and holding him close. Comforting him. Her cold smile as she touched Twig's broken hand. It wasn't just animals who could change.

Ben flipped his hood up and strode out of the stable, willing himself not to run.

"Ben," Mr. Murley called, "grab my measuring tape from the shed, will you please?"

Ben didn't turn around. "Sure," he said.

"The yellow thing with all the little lines and numbers," Twig said.

"I know."

Halfway to the shed, Ben almost changed course and bolted into the woods. But he couldn't leave without Indy. No, he'd wait until later. He knew why Mr. Murley wanted that measuring tape—to figure out how far to expand the stable. Soon enough the Murleys would have one less unicorn to worry about stabling. Ben wasn't sure where he was going to go, but it had to be somewhere they'd never find him.

A familiar sound interrupted Ben's thoughts. Hooves pounding. Not the soft thump of the ponies in the pasture, but the bump-crunch of the gravel road. A tall figure leap-galloped down the road, headed right for the gate, cloak billowing in the light, misty rain. A crack of light shone through the clouds, making him glimmer like something unreal. Something unworldly. No, just something from another world—Terracornus.

CHAPTER 28

IT HAD BEEN SO long since Ben had seen Merrill ride—really ride. The unicorn stallion looked steady and proud, as did his rider. Merrill pulled Marble back at the driveway gate and waited. The unicorn was looking well—very well.

"Twig!" Ben called over his shoulder as he ran for the gate. "He's here! It's Merrill!"

Merrill dismounted and walked Marble through the gate. The unicorn sniffed and called out to the stable. A chorus of greetings from Wonder, Indy, and Bounce replied. A smattering of nervous pony whinnies joined the mix.

Merrill tipped his head toward the stable, listening with the trained ear of a lifelong herder. "You have another unicorn in there, Ben-boy?"

"We took Bounce in," he said. "She's still healing."

"Merrill!" Twig reached them, out of breath. She brushed the stray, wet blond hair out of her face. "Is everything all right? What are you doing here?"

"Don't worry, Twig-girl. Things are going to be just fine, I think. Thought it was about time I met these ranch Murleys. Besides"—his smile wobbled a little—nervously?—as he gave Marble a pat—"this isn't my only surprise."

"He's all better!" Twig exclaimed.

But Ben said, "What do you mean?"

Before Merrill could answer, Mr. Murley emerged from the stable.

"Ben? Is this…"

Ben nodded. "Merrill, this is my uncle, David Murley."

"Pleasure to meet you, Mr. Murley."

The men shook hands. Mr. Murley grinned, his face animated with boyish curiosity.

Merrill's smile was of a different sort. He looked at Mr. Murley from one angle and then the other. "I'm sorry." The old herder cleared his throat. "There's a resemblance, you know. To Darian."

There was? Ben had never really thought about it, but then, he'd been accustomed to seeing Mr. Murley when Father was still alive. When he and his father were secretly keeping an eye on the ranch.

"I wish we could've met. He must have been a fine man to raise this boy. We all love Ben."

Ben ducked his head and tried not to cry. Why? Why did Mr. Murley's kind words make him feel even more lost?

"Merrill, why don't you come in and meet my wife and the rest of the girls?"

By the time Ben helped Merrill settle Marble in one of the pasture shelters, the porch was full of girls, watching in fascination.

Ben shot Merrill an apologetic look, but he smiled warmly as he shook each girl's hand.

He pulled off his wet woolen cap as he greeted Mrs. Murley. "Thanks for taking in this boy, feeding him something decent for a change."

"I eat decent!" Ben protested.

"Mrs. M's food is better than decent," Janessa said. "You'll see. It's almost lunch. You can stay for lunch, can't you, Mr. Merrill?"

"Yes!" Twig said. "We're having chicken and dumpling soup. You have to stay."

"Well, that's up to—"

"Of course," Mrs. Murley said. "Come in and get dry, and we'll all have lunch."

•••

Lunch had been eaten, and Twig sat around the table with Ben and Merrill and the rest of the family, sipping hot chocolate—her suggestion. Merrill wiped an extra mustache of whipped cream from his face. Casey giggled, and Merrill gave her a wink.

The old herder slipped his hand into his coat and drew out a piece of paper. "I have a letter for you, David. And Laura." He nodded at Mrs. Murley. "It's from the boy's mother."

"What?!" Ben almost dropped his mug of hot chocolate.

Twig spat a mouthful back into her cup.

"It seems she has more to say about this duel of yours."

Mr. Murley took the letter and unfolded it in front of Mrs. Murley.

Mrs. Murley brought her hand to her mouth. She looked up at Ben. "This is signed, 'Her Majesty, the Queen of Westland.'"

"That's her," Merrill said matter-of-factly.

Ben was silent. Mr. Murley turned his questioning look to Twig.

She nodded. "Ben's a prince." She spoke quietly, but that didn't make it less noticeable. Janessa squealed with excitement.

"Not the crown prince," Ben said.

"That's his brother, Griffin."

"You have a brother?" Regina said.

"He's too old for you." Twig gave her a poke.

"He's no good anyway!"

"Ben!" Twig said.

"Blast Griffin!" Ben stuffed his fists under the table. He looked just about ready to bash something.

Janessa and Casey gasped. The Murleys and Merrill joined Twig in giving Ben looks of disapproval.

"Sorry," Ben muttered. "Not good enough for any of you, anyway."

Regina grinned at that. She batted her thick, dark eyelashes. Twig kicked her under the table, hard this time.

"Ow!"

"Girls," Mrs. Murley warned. *We have guests*, her look reminded them.

Mr. Murley cleared his throat. "Let's see what...Her Majesty...has to say. And then maybe Ben can explain how a Murley came to be a prince of Westland." Mr. Murley's smile shook a little with the strangeness of it.

"I'm not surprised a Murley would be royalty," Taylor said.

Mandy rolled her eyes.

Mrs. Murley picked up the letter. "She says, 'I understand that you are relatives of my late husband, Darian—may his soul soar with the spirits of unicorns—and that you have taken in my wayward son, Ben.'"

Mrs. Murley hesitated at the word *wayward*. She glanced at Ben.

He was steaming mad, and Twig couldn't help being angry on his behalf. "She's the one who's wayward. Her men did this to my hand. And she put us in the dungeon!"

There were gasps all around the table. Oh no. Stupid Twig. She'd said too much.

"What is that, another one of Casey's stories?" Regina snorted. Mandy gave her own scornful laugh.

But Casey said, "The dungeon!" and looked like she was going to cry.

"Ben?" Mrs. Murley said.

"It's true," said Merrill. "But go on, please. Read the letter. Then Ben and I will explain the rest."

What would be left to explain? The queen would tell the Murleys to stop Ben from going to the Death Swamp. She'd ruin their plans. She might even insist they send him back. And she *was* Ben's mother. The Murleys might not send him back to her, but they wouldn't go against his mother's wishes to let him do something she said would endanger his life.

"Don't listen to her!" Twig banged her fist on the table. "She *wants* war with Eastland."

"Twig," Mr. Murley said, "I don't know where all that is coming from, but this is what Ben's mother says: 'I know my son and how determined he can be. So like his father, with his noble ideas. So we will let him ride into the Death Swamp. He may not win his duel, but I assure you, no harm will come to him. I will see to that.'"

"What?"

"She's negotiated a slight change in the terms of the duel with the Prince of Eastland. Each dueler will have one companion. An adult, to make sure they're safe."

"Who?"

"One of her guards, she says."

Someone like Neal. Twig exchanged looks with Ben.

Why? Why had she changed her mind? Why had she writ-ten to help convince the Murleys to let Ben go?

CHAPTER 29

THE SUN SHONE ON Twig's jacket. It was a warm spring day, and she longed to take it off, but the swamp lay just ahead, green and shadowy. Wet and teeming with bugs— and much, much worse. Her mini-backpack was safe under her bright red shell. On her back was her bow and quiver. The queen had promised her safe passage in and out of Terracornus for the event, but still, after Ben went into the Death Swamp, she'd be all alone.

Merrill was supposed to be here. He'd been granted the same pass, yet he hadn't met them by the passage tree as they'd planned. They'd sent Emmie with a message, but she'd come back to them with it still in the little tube attached to her leg, unopened.

The queen was there with her entourage. A handful of Eastlanders stood by as well, to ensure fair play.

The queen gave Twig and Ben a tight smile. "Neal will accompany you through the swamp, Ben."

Ben nodded stoically, but Twig couldn't help a grimace of

distaste. She didn't trust Neal or the queen. What if they were up to something? What if it had something to do with Merrill not being here?

"Neal can help me carry this." Ben pointed to the pirogue they'd set down behind them. "It's not heavy; Twig and I can carry it. But it does take two."

"A boat?" the Eastlanders murmured. "What are they doing with a boat?"

The Queen of Westland stepped forward. She looked from the pirogue at Ben and Twig's feet to Ben's face. For an instant she looked stricken, near panic.

"What are you doing with that boat, my son?" The calm was as forced as the smile.

"We've decided not to take the boardwalk, Mother. We'll go through the swamp in a pirogue—this boat—instead."

The most senior member of the Eastland party cleared his throat. "Just a minute there." He took out a piece of paper and followed the lines of script with a crooked finger. Finally he looked up and shook his head. "There is no rule against it."

"Let me see that," one of the women from his group said. "Whatever they can carry. It says so right here. The contestant, one companion, one unicorn each, and whatever they can carry."

"But they have to ride in, don't they?" A middle-aged Eastlander tugged at his beard in agitation.

The woman's nut-brown hair bobbed as she shook her head. "It's not in the rules."

"But it's tradition! What will Prince Reynald say? We have a responsibility."

Her face twisted in a smirk. "Prince Reynald would say let them have their boat. Let them try to traverse the Death Swamp by water."

"The swamp will do his work for him," the bearded man agreed grimly.

"It will be disappointing, I'm sure, not to have a fight. But one way or another, Reynald wins this duel."

"You mean to say you are going to let these two paddle into the Death Swamp in this—this—canoe?" the queen said.

"It's a pirogue," Twig said.

"Ben," the queen said, "you must take the boardwalk. I insist on it."

Ben shook his head. "This is my duel, Mother."

"I'm afraid Neal will be unable to accompany you, then. If you go this way, then you go alone."

"No, he doesn't!" Twig's pulse pounded as she spoke up. She couldn't let Ben take that boardwalk and fight Reynald to the death. Though the duelers' companions weren't allowed to fight for them, they could assist them, help protect them from the dangers of the swamp. "He goes with me."

"With you?" the queen said.

Twig flexed her left hand. It was healed now. They'd practiced and planned and packed. But was she really ready to face the Death Swamp?

"Yes, I'll be his companion. I'll help him through the Death Swamp."

"Twig…" Ben looked at her, full of surprise and worry. If the Death Swamp didn't kill her, the Murleys would once they found out.

"I know that map by heart."

"I cannot let you—"

"You don't have a choice. We're partners, remember? We're the herders of Lonehorn Island." At least for a few more days, when Daddy would come home and she'd have to leave Wonder, the ranch, everything.

He nodded slowly, understanding. "Partners."

The queen gave them a cold, hard look. Then she turned her back on them and walked away.

"Is she going to stop us?" Twig whispered to Ben.

"She cannot. Not now. She's already agreed to the duel. She gave her word."

"She's not happy."

"She'll never be happy with me."

From the other side of the swamp, a long horn blast sounded.

"Eastland is ready. Come on, Twig. We're going to beat

Reynald there and take his flag before he makes it halfway through the Death Swamp."

Twig couldn't help smiling. Finally, Ben believed in the plan she and the girls had come up with. Even if it was only because his mother opposed it. Ben was determined to win and keep the Death Swamp from winning any of their lives while they were at it.

"Ben!" Griffin grabbed his arm and hissed. "You cannot do this. It will never work. Just take the boardwalk, please."

"I have a better chance this way."

"You have no chance! Do you understand? No chance at all!"

From the other side of the swamp, the horn sounded again. Ben said, "Ready."

It was Griffin's job to blow the ram's horn. Flames of anger shot from his eyes like the blue fire in the stories of the Death Swamp, but he raised it to his mouth and blew.

Twig shot Griffin a reproachful look, slipped Wonder's lead around her wrist, and grabbed her end of the pirogue.

Twig and Ben lifted the boat together and headed for the entrance to the Death Swamp. Emmie circled over the crowd, then landed on top of the pirogue. Indy and Wonder neighed their distaste and confusion as Twig and Ben tethered them to a tree at the edge of the swamp. Twig's arms shook as she balanced the edge of the pirogue on her shoulder. She felt the load lighten a little as Ben put some more muscle—more than his share—into lifting the other side of the boat.

Emmie launched into the air, high above the treetops. Twig hoped she wouldn't go far. She liked to think they'd keep some connection with the world outside the swamp, even if it was just one small emerald pigeon.

Twig took the first step off the sticky but still mostly solid ground and onto the boardwalk. The boards were gray, the gray of death. Bright green foam seeped up between them— not the brightness of life—the brightness of toxic stuff that could end it.

They carried the pirogue a few yards in, then carefully stepped to one side and lowered it to the boardwalk. Twig's hands were still shaking. She felt something wet. A blob of green foam. She shook her hand, flinging it into the swamp.

"It's just algae," Ben reminded her. "Touching the water won't hurt you."

Twig nodded, glad she'd held back that yelp. If things were anything like Earth here, then she only had to worry about the water getting into any cuts and scrapes and causing infection.

They turned the pirogue over and slowly lowered it into the water. Ben held it still against the boardwalk while Twig fetched Wonder.

"You get in first, Twig."

She stepped in, Wonder's lead in hand. She smiled steadily

and looked into Wonder's eyes. "Wonder-girl, we're going for a little ride. Look what I have for you." Twig showed Wonder the lump of sugar, a rare treat. "Come on."

Wonder stepped into the boat, then lost her nerve and tried to bounce back out. The boat lurched with her sudden movement, and Wonder splashed into the water.

The boat drifted a few inches, then stopped, stuck in the mud. Thank God the water was only a few inches deep. But Wonder snorted and shook her head. Twig groped in the ooze for her lead. If Wonder bolted into the swamp—

Ben stretched across the boardwalk on his belly, trying to grab the boat. "Use the paddle, Twig. I cannot reach it."

Twig held the lead tight with one hand and took the paddle in the other. She pushed off the mud with it, and Ben grasped the side of the pirogue and drew it back. Wonder wanted to follow. She scrambled back into the boat. Twig talked her into sitting down so she could pet her and still reach the ground with the paddle.

It wasn't so hard to get Indy into the pirogue once Wonder was there, though he made it clear how unhappy he was about it. He glared at Ben, then at Wonder for getting in first. The unicorns had a little discussion. Both of them were on their feet and looking ready to jump. They had to do something or they were never going to get on their way. Already the Boy King had a head start.

"Push!" Twig cried. "Quick!"

They both pushed the pirogue off and into deeper water before their unicorns could make their escape. The pirogue cut through the water, smooth and quiet and quick. Twig allowed herself a smile. They were on their way. They were going to do this.

Overhead, a bright green blur wove in and out of view. As though to offer them extra reassurance, Emmie cooed. Her call bounced off the swamp life, sounding like more than just one bird. Not alone.

Mrs. Murley often told Twig she was never alone. But she and Ben would be, until they made it to the other side of the swamp. Even then, would there be a friendly face to welcome them? Would Merrill make it? The group from Westland would be hurrying around the swamp right now to meet them. Only a small delegation from each side would remain by its entrance to be witnesses.

Twig took her sketchbook from her mini-backpack and wrote a quick note. "Ben, see if you can call Emmie back. I want to try to send a message one more time."

The cooed answer to Ben's whistle was barely audible. But in a moment, the letter pigeon arrived. Twig rolled her note up tight. It was addressed to everyone. Merrill, the Murleys, Casey, her parents, explaining what she'd done, apologizing. Telling them she loved them. Just in case.

The swamp was almost peaceful, and the smell wasn't so bad now that Twig had gotten used to it. Lulled by the gliding of the boat, Wonder and Indy rested. Maybe all the stories were exaggerations, tales grown taller over time.

"Pull to the left," Ben said. Even he sounded at ease as they navigated around a cluster of tree roots that jutted into their path, arching high above the water. Twig followed the roots with her eyes, up to the trunk, into the dangling branches. They were strangely dark, the lichen blackish. Mist hovered over the water—not the mist of Lonehorn Island, but a brownish gloom.

Ben took in a sharp breath. "This is it, Twig," he whispered. "The heart of the Death Swamp."

CHAPTER 30

WONDER WHINED, AND INDY huffed at Ben. "It's all right, Indy-boy." Ben gave each of the unicorns another lump of sugar.

"You steer," Twig said. "I'll get out the map."

Twig scratched Wonder with one hand and traced their route from the boardwalk to the true heart of the Death Swamp with the other.

The dangers leaped off the page, tongues of fire and gnashing teeth. *We're here. We're everywhere. And now we've got you, Twig. We're going to take you from that island for good.*

One wrong turn, and they could go up in smoke or be sucked—or dragged—into the mud, becoming a part of it forever. No one she loved would ever see her again. She thought of Mom, alone in jail. Twig knew her mother missed her, that she longed to see her. And Daddy would be home in a few days. He was looking forward to coming to see her at the ranch, watching her ride before he took her home with him.

The swamp haze grew thicker, the shadows darker. Twig

got out the big flashlight she'd packed and flipped it on. Ben gripped her arm and pointed. She stifled a scream. Scattered above the water, small, round lights glowed red.

"Swamp lizards," Ben whispered.

"Those are their eyes? There are so many of them."

"We'll stay still and calm. We'll be okay, I think." Ben pushed his paddle gently away from the glowing eyes. Twig did the same, trying not to make a splash.

Wonder shrieked. Twig jumped up to steady her, and that's when she saw the snake creeping along Wonder's back, wriggling through her mane. She recognized the pattern of stripes instantly from the illustrations on the map. It lifted its pointed head, poised to pierce Wonder's neck.

Before Twig could draw her sword, Indy slashed at the snake with his horn and sliced it in two. But as he did so, he lost his balance and plunged into the water. Wonder leaped after him. Ben tossed the writhing remains of the snake over the other side of the boat and whistled for Indy to come back, but Wonder was spooked. She leaped farther away from the snake—and the pirogue.

Indy called to Wonder and turned back toward the boat and his rider. Twig held the flashlight up just in time to see a pair of those red eyes darting through the water, right toward Indy. Ben yelled a warning, and Indy leaped and swam away, after Wonder.

"Paddle!" Ben cried. "Hurry!"

They paddled furiously after the unicorns and away from the dozen or so red eyes—eyes that gleamed with new interest. One by one, the swamp lizards began to weave through the swamp plants toward the little boat.

Twig called to Wonder, and Ben whistled to Indy, and their unicorns struggled against the swamp, back to the pirogue. Ben grabbed Indy by the halter. He pulled while Indy lunged. Indy made it in, but the pirogue tipped with the impact. Twig shoved her paddle into the muck, and Ben shifted his weight, steadying it just before it tipped over. Ben scooped swamp water out of the pirogue with cupped hands while Twig tried to calm Wonder and get her to come to the boat.

"Nice and steady. Come on." Wonder slowed down all right. Now she was barely moving at all, and the near capsizing of the pirogue had reignited the swamp lizards' interest. Wonder snorted and tossed her head. She kicked, and Twig saw it—a tangle of swamp weeds wrapped around her foreleg.

"Wonder's in trouble!"

The unicorn lunged forward, toward the boat—into a dip in the swamp floor, into deeper water. She sank up to her neck, her eyes wild with fear, pleading with Twig, *Save me. Save me. Don't let me die here.* Ben struggled to keep Indy under control and in the boat. Twig threw everything off her back, even her shell and her mini-backpack. Holding only her sword, she jumped into the water and swam to Wonder.

Ben was shouting at her. An arrow whizzed by, and something splashed. Something big. A swamp lizard's bumpy tail disappeared into the water.

Twig groped for Wonder's reins and tried to hold her head still so she could talk to her. Wonder was growing more and more exhausted. Sinking deeper and deeper. And it was impossible to hold on to Wonder with one hand and her sword with the other while treading water. Twig took a deep breath, let go of Wonder, and dove into the murky water. She felt for Wonder, praying she wouldn't take a hoof in the head or accidentally slash Wonder with her sword.

She found Wonder's leg and worked her fingers under the weeds that threatened to tether her to the Death Swamp forever. There was no way she could cut them off Wonder's leg with her sword without cutting Wonder too. Not the way the unicorn was kicking and fighting to escape, to stay alive.

Desperately, Twig slashed through the water underneath Wonder's feet. The water surged around her, and Twig bobbed up, gasping and spitting swampy grit. Wonder swam toward the pirogue. She was free. Twig had cut the weeds away from the swamp floor.

"Twig!" Ben held his hand out for her, and she climbed into the pirogue.

Twig held on to Wonder's bridle while Ben pushed the

pirogue into shallower water, and Wonder clambered in. Ragged weeds hung from her forelegs.

Ben glanced behind them at the swamp lizards. He shoved a paddle at Twig. "Let's go!"

Still out of breath, Twig paddled for her life—for all of their lives. They navigated around a cluster of floating plants that resembled blackened lily pads and into a patch of open water.

"Strange." Ben took Twig's flashlight and shined it. "They're not following."

The pairs of red eyes clustered together, watching but not following—almost as though they were waiting. For what?

A burst of blue flame lit up the swamp. The unicorns cried out, and this time, Twig couldn't stop her scream.

"Swamp fire! Twig, the map!" Ben pushed them away from the flames. "We've gotten off course. We have to get out of here and headed the right direction without—" He nodded at the swamp lizards.

Without running right back into their hungry, razor-toothed mouths.

CHAPTER 31

TWIG HASTILY UNROLLED THE map. She scanned it, then found the spot they'd entered—Fire Lagoon. "I think I know where—"

"Ahh!"

Flames shot up, bright blue, just off the starboard side of the pirogue. Fire crawled along Ben's cloak. Twig helped him tear it off and smother the flames. The side of the pirogue was singed. Wonder and Indy neighed wildly and moved to the opposite side of the boat. It tipped dangerously low in the water.

Twig and Ben struggled to keep the unicorns calm and the pirogue balanced as they paddled through the minefield of bursting flame. Finally they reached the end of the lagoon and a narrow passage of water that led them in the right direction. Ben put down his paddle with a sigh of relief. He grimaced at his blackened cloak, then put it back on.

Twig hugged Wonder and said a prayer of thanks. She'd almost lost her. They'd almost lost everything.

Twig consulted the map again. "The good news, aside from

the fact that we made it through there alive, is that little detour through Fire Lagoon was actually a shortcut. We never would've gone through there on purpose, but I think it saved us some of that time we lost with Wonder being stuck. Look."

She pointed out the swamp life, beginning to look more like life instead of death again—green instead of black and rotting, the mud brown instead of tarlike. As long as they stayed on course, the worst was over. They headed toward the boardwalk. Soon they'd be on solid ground, they'd have that flag, and everyone could go home in peace.

"There's the boardwalk," Ben said.

"I think we're close to the Eastland entrance. Pull up to the boardwalk, and I'll check."

Ben pushed the pirogue to the boardwalk and used his paddle to hold it steady while Twig climbed out. She peered through the binoculars Taylor had loaned her, down the rickety path, into the fog of swamp fumes. At first she couldn't make anything out, but then the haze shifted, and she glimpsed something bright green, trimmed in gold.

"There! There it is! Eastland's flag."

They got their unicorns out of the pirogue and onto the boardwalk, then lifted the boat out of the water and set it down.

Twig mounted Wonder, then turned back to look at the flag. Though it hung limp in the gloom of the Death Swamp, it was the most beautiful thing she'd seen in a long time. But this time Twig spotted something under the flag. She lowered the binoculars with a shaky hand.

"Oh no. Oh, Ben. He's here."

"What?" Ben took the binoculars and looked for himself. His frown of worry turned to fury. "Reynald! He's brought that soldier, Ackley, with him as his companion."

The figures walked slowly back and forth on a little section of boardwalk. Pacing. Waiting—for them.

Reynald didn't seem to notice them yet. He and Ackley had no binoculars, and the swamp smells must be keeping the unicorns from catching one another's scents. They were hundreds of yards away, but Twig talked to Wonder, urging her to be still, not to cause any vibrations on the boardwalk.

"How did he know?" Twig whispered just in case.

"That bird! Just when we entered the swamp, I thought I heard Emmie cooing to another pigeon. The Eastlanders sent Reynald a message as soon as they saw our boats. He's been here the whole time, waiting for us."

"But he'd never get our flag first by waiting here."

"He'd keep us from getting his. Reynald wasn't willing to bet that the swamp would kill us. Besides, he wants a fight. He thinks he'll take care of us, and then take his time riding through the swamp to get my flag."

"What are we going to do?"

"Fight for that flag. Get ready, Twig."

The boardwalk groaned under the unicorns' hooves as they advanced. Soon Reynald and his companion would know they were coming. *Dear God*, Twig prayed, *don't let us die. Don't let me have to kill anyone. Not a unicorn or a person.*

The unicorns neighed. All heads turned toward the sound. Another rider was coming from the south side of the swamp. He glanced quickly at them, then plunged forward, toward Reynald. As he rode, he fired at Reynald. Though he was covered in swamp muck, Twig recognized those movements. They were so much like Ben's. There was only one person it could be.

Griffin.

He was headed for the boardwalk. To cut off the Boy King's charge. To stop the duel.

Where did he come from? But as his mud-spattered mount plowed through the swamp, Twig knew the answer. He'd entered from the north side of the swamp. He hadn't used the boardwalk at all; he'd just ridden right through.

"Griffin! No!" Ben plunged off the boardwalk, headed for Griffin, shouting, "She sent you, didn't she? To stop me. I should've known she'd never really agree!"

"Get back on the boardwalk! I'm not doing this for her! I'm doing it because I cannot lose you, Ben."

The boardwalk shook. In the distance, Stone Heart and Ackley's unicorn howled for battle. They charged toward Twig while Ben and Griffin splashed and argued in the murky water.

CHAPTER 32

A LUMP SWELLED IN BEN'S throat even as his pulse pounded with urgency. His brother and his unicorn, Breaker, were in a terrible state. A trickle of blood streamed through the mud and algae caked on Griffin's unicorn's coat. A nasty scrape marred Griffin's cheek, and his cloak was ripped almost in half. His quiver was dangerously close to empty. He drew his sword—or what was left of it. The end of it had broken—or been bitten—right off.

"This is my decision." Ben cut in front of Griffin. "It has nothing to do with you."

Griffin veered to the side. "No, it was *my* decision, and it has everything to do with me."

Ackley fired at Griffin, and all he could do was dodge. Ben fired back. Out of the corner of his eye, he saw Twig, all alone on the boardwalk, charging bravely toward the Boy King. Her courage would be no match for Reynald's skill. Ben made his choice. He left Griffin and headed for the boardwalk to help Twig.

Griffin had ruined everything Ben was trying to do. Now

the unicorns would suffer the losses of another war. Griffin had made it this far, winning who knew how many battles against the swamp—and now he was going to die. But Twig shouldn't have to pay the price.

"What is this?" the Boy King shrieked as he fired, not at Twig, but at Griffin. "What kind of cheating? What kind of trickery?"

Though stricken by the sound of the arrow piercing his brother's shoulder, of Griffin's strangled cry, Ben still felt the shame of Reynald's words, of what Griffin had done. Griffin drew his last arrow and, with a shout of agony, fired at Reynald.

"Ben! Behind you!" Twig cried.

There was a great splash, a flash of enormous teeth. A snap. Ben whirled toward his brother and grabbed at whatever he could. He pulled Griffin off Breaker just as the stallion disappeared under the water in the grip of a swamp lizard.

The putrid water bubbled up, then stilled. Ben clutched his older brother to his chest with all his strength as Griffin called out desperately for Breaker.

"He's gone, Griff."

And now we're all going to die. A sticky wetness coated Ben's hand—Griffin's blood, dripping into the swamp water as he hung half on, half off Indy in front of Ben. "Get behind me," Ben commanded. For once, Griffin listened.

"They're coming. Look!" Twig cried. Sets of lizard eyes

glided above the water, leaving telltale wakes behind them. "They look so big."

A swamp lizard launched out of the water, right onto the boardwalk, and snapped at Wonder's feet. The boardwalk groaned with the force of the swamp lizard's lunge and the pounding of Wonder's hooves. Ben watched in horror as the section of boards gave way and crashed into the shallows of the swamp. The lizard attacked relentlessly, and beautiful Wonder Light splashed into the muck.

Wonder kicked. She struck the lizard in the head, then leaped farther into the water to escape its thrashing. Indy lunged and slashed through the lizard's throat with his horn. It sank into the swamp, limp and lifeless—but the swamp teemed with movement.

"Reynald!" Ben said. The boardwalk had collapsed beneath the Boy King, and now he was wading through the swamp too. "We have to work together if we want to get out of here. If we want to live."

"I'm to trust you after this?" Reynald plucked Griffin's arrow from the hood of his cloak, where it had lodged after narrowly missing his head.

"I had no part in it," Ben told him.

But Twig said, "You don't have a choice!"

Reynald let his arrow fly, right at Twig. Wonder leaped aside just in time, and behind Ben, Griffin grunted and something else flew—Griffin's dagger. It just missed Reynald's ear and struck Ackley instead.

Ackley plunged backward into the water. A frenzy of snapping and gnashing surrounded him. Twig screamed.

"Stay calm!" Ben barely got out the words.

Stone Heart flew into a panic as the mass of hungry jaws stirred up the water around his nimble feet, and his rider cried out in horror. He reared, and Reynald fought to stay on, but he was no match for the power of Stone Heart's terror.

The Boy King soared through the air and skid-splashed to a landing on a mass of water plants just out of reach of the swamp lizards.

"Look out!" Twig cried.

As Reynald scrambled backward across the slippery swamp plants, a wake shot toward him like an arrow. Twig darted around, circled behind the swamp lizards, and tried to make her way to Reynald, to save him, even though he'd just tried to shoot her.

The lizard's massive head broke out of the water, jaws poised to crush Reynald's legs and drag him to his death, but Ben's arrow struck right between his reptilian eyes. The beast fell into the water with a splash.

Twig leaned down, barely hanging on to Wonder. She extended her hand. Reynald took it and climbed behind her. Wonder scrambled onto what remained of the boardwalk.

"Stone Heart," Reynald said hoarsely. "Please, help him."

Ben met Reynald's pleading eyes. He nodded. "Hang on, Griff."

"Ben!" Twig said. That was all. But her eyes said the rest. *Don't die.*

Ben said, "Just keep shooting. Keep me covered."

"Get close." Griffin's voice was barely audible in Ben's ear. "I can take Stone Heart. I can ride."

"Griff—"

Another swamp lizard flew toward them through the water. It lunged out of the water. Just as Ben cried out, Twig's arrow pierced its head right between the eyes.

"Just do it," Griffin said. "I got us into this. Let me do the right thing. For once, just let me do it, Ben!"

So Ben rode, plowing through the swamp while Twig's arrows whizzed through the air. He drew alongside Stone Heart, who was stuck in a tangle of mud and swamp plants, struggling madly and getting nowhere. Griffin clambered onto Stone Heart's back.

Ben threw Indy's reins to Griffin so that he could hang on while Indy tried to pull Stone Heart free. "Go! Indy, yah!"

Griffin clung to Stone Heart with his legs as he groped in his pockets with his free hand.

"What are you doing?" Ben said.

"Hold on. Just a minute." Griffin pulled a tiny wooden tube out. He put it to his mouth and began to blow.

"What are you *doing*!"

Griffin moved his head as though in time with music, but no sound came out of the strange little instrument. He'd completely lost his mind. Or maybe he'd just lost too much blood. Ben reached out to snatch the little pipe and maybe smack some sense back into Griffin, but he froze halfway through the motion.

Stone Heart had grown still and quiet. He'd stopped his frantic struggling against the pull of the swamp. Underneath him, Ben felt the pulse of excitement, the tenseness of the battle, fade from Indy's body. Griffin motioned for Ben to drive Indy forward.

"Let's go, Indy-boy. Pull hard."

The mud squelched as Indy leaped and lunged and Stone Heart was wrenched free, calm and steady, no longer fighting against Indy's efforts. Griffin tossed Indy's reins back to Ben. He pulled Stone Heart in front, and without being told, Indy followed. He climbed up onto the boardwalk after Stone Heart—as though in a trance.

Hypnotized, that was the word Twig had used. Griffin had entranced the unicorns with that little instrument. Griffin was the unicorn thief.

CHAPTER 33

TWIG AND BEN FIRED arrow after arrow, until the water was still and the last of the swamp lizards had retreated. All the while Ben kept glancing at Griffin and battling his disgust. It really *was* all Griff's fault. Everything. And now Griffin had Indy under his control.

Griffin dismounted and handed Stone Heart over to Reynald. Reynald took the reins gratefully. He turned his full attention to his beloved Stone Heart.

"What is that thing?" Twig whispered to Griffin, casting a glance at Reynald. But Reynald's face was buried in Stone Heart's mane.

"A unicorn whistle. It was my father's. Passed down from another herder who mentored him." He stroked the wood. "One of a kind. A secret few herders knew. He kept it closely guarded, seldom used."

"Because it isn't right!" Twig hissed. "Controlling them like that—it isn't right."

"Wake them up," Ben said stonily. "Bring them back."

Ben pretended not to see the tear cutting through the grime on Griffin's face. His brother blew the whistle, moving as though to music. Music none of them could hear. The unicorns stirred. They whinnied and sniffed and pawed at the ground. They realized where they were and neighed anxiously again, but this time there were no swamp lizards to send them into a panic, and their riders took control.

A strange smile curled Reynald's mouth. He mounted Stone Heart and headed down the boardwalk, toward his flag.

"What's he doing?" Twig said. "Does he still want a fight?"

"Let him go. Even if we fought him for it and won, it wouldn't be ours." Ben glared at Griffin. "We broke the rules."

Griffin stood there alone, his unicorn gone. He held the unicorn whistle out to Ben. "He'd want you to have it. You were the one he trusted."

Not with this secret. His father had never said a word about it. Neither had Merrill. Why? Couldn't something like this have helped them deal with Dagger? Couldn't it have saved his father's life?

Ben shook his head at Griffin's offering, feeling sick.

"He didn't give it to me." Griffin looked beyond sick. "I'm sorry. I took it, and I never got to tell him I'm sorry. I saw him use it when I was little. Before everything changed. When all I ever wanted to be was a herder just like him. He used to practice on a little flute. An ordinary one that made music we could hear. Don't you remember, Ben? Don't you remember the songs?"

"He played music," Ben said, "by the fire. To pass the time."

"No, not just to pass the time. When I saw him use this on a crazed unicorn, I recognized the pattern. Even though I couldn't hear a sound, I recognized the movement of his fingers, the tune. I knew I had to have it. I could be a great herder if only I could use it."

"So you *stole* it?" Twig said.

Ben jumped down from Indy. He advanced on Griffin. "When? How long have you had this?"

"About ten years."

Ben swallowed hard over the realization. "He never mentioned it because there was no point. It was gone, and we had to deal with Dagger without it. He's dead! He's dead because you took it!"

Twig leaped between them, and Ben realized his hand was clenched around his knife.

"Darian died because of Dagger," Twig said. She grabbed Ben's cloak and looked into his eyes. Hers were full of tears.

Ben pulled away. He looked down at his weapon. At his hand, white with the fierceness of his grip—of Dagger's grip on him still.

"Dagger killed him, and no one else. It was wrong, Ben, what Griffin did. It was wrong, but you have to forgive him."

Indy whinnied his concern. He nuzzled Ben's back. Ben tossed his dagger into the swamp. He turned his back on Griffin. "I cannot." He put a hand on Indy's neck, but he couldn't even look into his unicorn's quicksilver eyes. The eyes that would draw him back. He was far away. He wanted to be far away from everything.

"He's right, you know," Griffin said to Twig. "It's my fault. So many things are my fault. This. You being in this swamp. It's my fault."

"Griffin," Twig said. "Your mother wanted you to wait by the boardwalk and take Reynald and Ackley out, didn't she?"

"She only agreed to this because I was supposed to take one of the side passages near Eastland's entrance," Griffin replied. "I was supposed to sneak up on Reynald and take care of him before he ever set eyes on Ben. We'd get the flag, and Ben would have no choice but to come out of the swamp with it. My mother would get rid of Reynald, and Ben would get what he wanted—the truce with Eastland upheld—and he'd still be alive. She cannot stand the thought of losing Ben."

"And you couldn't either. That's why, when you realized we'd be going through the swamp by boat, you came anyway."

"My mother told me there was nothing I could do about Ben trying to boat through the swamp. She wanted me to stick with eliminating Reynald. She wouldn't risk having both of her sons killed. She told Neal to go with me." He turned to Ben. "But I wanted to find you. To protect you. I broke away from Neal as soon as I could—when we ran into a nasty nest of swamp lizards. I don't know what happened to him." He shook his head. "After that, the swamp had its own ideas about which way I should go. When I couldn't find you, and I realized I was near Eastland's entrance, I cut through to the main boardwalk. I knew that Reynald would be there waiting. He's not the only one who has spies. I was afraid I'd be too late."

"Unfortunately," Ben said through gritted teeth, "you weren't."

"Ben," Twig said.

It was just a whisper, just his name, but it stirred another whisper in Ben's heart. *This is how you honor your father. Forgive.*

Ben turned around to face Griffin. Griffin saw Ben's face and crumpled to his knees on the rickety boardwalk. He stared at the water as though he might as well just fall in.

"You started this whole thing by taking unicorns. You let her think it was Eastland."

"I never thought Eastland would be blamed! I was trying to save the unicorns. To start rebuilding the herds—and building up the power to resist what she's been doing. What could I do?"

"You could've told the truth," Twig said. "Once you found out Ben was going to pay for it."

"I tried to stop him. I—"

"You took Indy!" Ben said. "He didn't need saving. None of that is true!"

Griffin's eyes snapped up—blue like their mother's. "I took him to bring you back. One of Father's tunnels goes under part of the swamp. I took him through it, to my hideout. I thought you'd go to Mother, not track him there! I needed you here. I'm supposed to be king. Next year, I'm supposed to be king."

"So?"

"So do you really think she'll let that happen? Didn't you ever wonder what would happen to me? To all of us?" Griffin shook his head. "Tell me you care about more than that island. Your herd. There are unicorns here who need you. People who need you. I needed you to care. I had to make you see. Make you face it. I knew you wouldn't care unless you realized it would affect you too, that your island wasn't immune."

"What are you trying to do, Griff?"

"I thought once she saw you…I thought Father would come with you, of course. I didn't know…how could you not tell me?"

"How could I? You saw what happened when I told Mother! What could I have done? Put it in a letter?"

Griffin's expression softened. "You don't put something like that in a letter."

"You don't keep it from your brother either," Ben said quietly. He sat down next to Griffin. "He loved you, you know. He wanted you with us. Every time he taught me something new, I could see it in his eyes. He was remembering teaching you."

"You're everything he wanted you to be, Ben. Everything he was."

"Not everything." Ben rose and held a hand out to his brother. Griffin took it, and Ben pulled him up, and then Griffin pulled him into a hug. "I'll forgive you, Griff. Somehow." Not just because it was what Ben knew his father would want, what his father would do, but because it was the right thing to do.

CHAPTER 34

TWIG EYED THE SWAMP-FILLED gap in the boardwalk. "Should we try to get back up on that side of the boardwalk and head back to Westland?"

"No. We owe Eastland an apology. Griff." Ben gestured for his brother to ride behind him, and they headed toward the Eastland entrance.

They'd survived the Death Swamp, and something even darker had been uncovered amid the muck and the rot—secrets that should never have been. For Ben, new pain on top of the old. And for Twig, painful old memories, bubbling up again. If Griffin had only told Ben what he wanted…

Ben never had a chance to know who his brother really was. And Twig was keeping the same kind of secret from her dad. But what choice did she have?

At the end of the boardwalk, Reynald was waiting. Waiting, and holding the flag of Eastland. "Come with me," he said.

They followed him out of the swamp. The Eastlanders and Westlanders had swapped sides to wait for their duelers to emerge. The Westlanders called out and clamored and pointed as they appeared. Among them, a large, muddy figure stood out—Neal had made it out of the swamp alive after all. Twig almost felt sorry for him, having to come out of the swamp and tell the queen both of her boys were still in there, missing. His hair was scorched, his clothing in shreds.

Twig saw the queen's anxious expression melt into relief at the sight of her sons. But soon she took on the confused look of all the others. What were both duelers doing here? Why did Reynald have his own flag and not Westland's?

In front of the onlookers, Reynald rode over to Ben. He held out the flag. "Take it," he said.

"But I didn't win."

"You saved my life. You earned this flag. I'll best you some other time—or, even better, in a few years, I'll best the new King of Westland."

A glint of new malice burned amid the gratitude. "But perhaps that's not fair, Griffin. You are a son, first and foremost. I suspect you were just doing what you were told." Boldly, he turned the glare right on the queen.

"I don't know what you're saying, but I do know you are not to be trusted. Your people stole from me—straight from my stable, even while you were a guest in my country, supposedly negotiating to extend our treaty!"

"Mother," Griffin said. "It was me."

"What was you?"

"I am the unicorn thief. I took Night Spark and all the others too."

"But…why?"

"I needed to be ready. To have my own forces for when I come of age."

"You thought I would oppose you?"

"Once you found out what I plan to do when I'm king, yes."

"And just what are you going to do?"

"Keep our defenses strong but avoid provoking war. Allow those who wish to do so to go back to herding."

"There are no unicorns left for them to herd." She waved her hand dismissively, as though that had nothing to do with her policies, as though it were unchangeable. "The war unicorns aren't suited to the wild."

"Eventually, some of them might be if the right people work with them. But there *is* one last herd. On Lonehorn Island. If they were protected, some of those unicorns might flourish again in Terracornus. Their numbers could build back up."

"I see." The queen smirked, but Twig wasn't buying it. She was scared and trying to hide it. The queen turned to the crowd. "And which of you support this?"

There was silence. Such a long silence. Twig wanted to grab Ben—and Griffin too—and run.

Ben opened his mouth to answer. But it just hung there. Open. He pointed behind Twig. She turned to see a group of riders approaching at a gallop. Two men on unicorns took the lead, and another rider on a larger mount was just behind them, followed by a row of five smaller figures and one riderless pony.

Rain Cloud.

Mr. Murley rode Bounce right alongside Merrill and Marble. Twig couldn't help beaming with pride, even as she worried what he would say, how angry he would be. Mr. Murley didn't ride with Merrill's ease just yet, but he was a good, strong rider. Another Murley, riding a unicorn, in Terracornus.

Mrs. Murley rode Feather, who couldn't quite keep up with the unicorns, and Rain Cloud just about kept up pace with her, urging the other ponies to hurry—Taylor and Chatterbox, Mandy and Sparkler, Regina and Celeste, Janessa and Gadget, Casey and Story.

The girls of Island Ranch formed a circle around Ben and Twig.

The queen turned to Ben. "Who," she said with a mocking smile, "is this?"

Rain Cloud snorted. His nostrils flared, and his ears pinned back.

Merrill cleared his throat and was about to introduce them, but Casey said, "Your Majesty, we're the people of the island. The island you wanted to forget."

The queen's face went white with rage. Her anger was a cold anger. So different from Ben's temper. *Oh no, Casey. Please, God,* Twig prayed, *don't let her say anything stupider.*

But it was the queen who spoke next. "Then you do not belong here."

Neal drew his sword, looking all too eager to take out his anger over being left in the Death Swamp on someone.

"Hey, now!" Merrill said.

"Yes we do belong here!" Casey shouted. "We're Twig's family, and Ben's too!"

To Twig's astonishment, the girls all cheered. Ben lifted his fist and cheered too.

"And one day we're going to be unicorn riders! All of us!"

Oh, Casey. Casey with her crazy stories. Twig looked into those big brown eyes. Full of dreams, yes. But full of determination too. The kind of determination that could make such dreams real.

This time, Twig was the first to shout. She raised her hand for Casey. "Riders!"

"Riders!" the others cheered. Ben too.

Mrs. Murley laughed out loud, a warm, teary laugh.

"The riders of Island Ranch," Mr. Murley agreed.

Casey dismounted and threw her arms around Twig. Before she knew it, she and Ben were in a huddle of hugs and prayers. Rain Cloud poked his nose in and made sure he got a hug of his own.

"I got your message," Merrill said to Twig. "That you were going into the Death Swamp with Ben." He shook his head. "I would've stopped you if I'd been here. I was delayed. Detained by the queen's men until they could verify my pass. By the time they let me go, Emmie found me. I knew it was too late to stop you, and I owed it to your family to tell them what was going on."

"Oh, Twig," Mrs. Murley said, "you're too brave for your own good."

"You all came," Twig said.

"We're in this together," Mr. Murley said. "We should've been all along."

Ben turned to the crowd. The queen's inner circle. Her finest soldiers. "And we should be too. Together, for the well-being of the unicorns. I faced the Death Swamp for all of us. For who we really are. You remember the days. You remember what it was to ride free. To watch over your herd, doing the same. You were herders, and Westland was free. We can be who we were—who we still are in our hearts—again!"

"I stand for Griffin. For the return of the herders!" Pete, Merrill's nephew, stepped forward.

"What's going on, Twig-girl?" Merrill said.

Quickly, Twig whispered an explanation. Merrill joined Pete. Then, one by one, many of the onlookers did the same. They were split, half left by the queen's side, half with Griffin.

"Well then," the queen said, "it seems the court of Westland has spoken, and they are divided."

"The *herders* of Westland have spoken," Griffin said. "They are not divided." He turned to his supporters. "I am humbled and honored. I don't deserve your allegiance. But with your help, when I am king, Westland will become a land of herders again."

"Perhaps, Griffin. We will see when that day comes." Though the queen smiled, the threat in her tone was undeniable. Her bright red tunic swished around her embroidered leggings as she turned her back on them. She cocked her head over her shoulder. "Go, Ben. Go back to your island with these people. With your father's people."

CHAPTER 35

TWIG SAT AT THE table, eying her drawing. She'd done this one on a piece of paper from a bigger drawing pad Keely had sent her. It took more space to capture such a moment—Twig and Ben on Wonder and Indy. Rain Cloud right beside Wonder. All the girls on their ponies, Mrs. Murley on Feather, Mr. Murley riding Bounce, and Merrill on Marble, just as they'd been, all together, in Terracornus.

It was time to stop staring at it. Time to stop fiddling with it and call it finished. Twig took a deep breath, then chose a dark green pencil and signed her name in the bottom right corner: Twig Tupper.

"Twig," Mrs. Murley called from the entryway, "there's something out here you should see."

Twig put down her colored pencil, gave her drawing one last glance, and went to the door. "What is it? Is Mr. Murley back from town?"

Mrs. Murley smiled. "He's back, and he brought you something."

Twig opened the door to the late spring sun, glittering on the grass, still wet from a morning rain. The pickup truck crunched over the gravel in the driveway. The passenger door flew open almost before the truck came to a stop, and a man in jeans and a new blue T-shirt got out.

"Twig!"

It had been so long since she'd heard her name in Daddy's voice, without the muffling of distance, the slight something's-in-between-us sound of a talk through Skype.

Twig ran to him, right into his open arms. She felt light, dizzy, and not just because her feet flew off the ground and he whirled her around. He set her down and cupped her face in his hands and kissed her.

"I know you don't like surprises, but I got in a day early, and Mr. Murley thought you'd like this one."

Twig just nodded through her tears, then threw her arms around him again. He held her for a long, long time. Finally she tipped her head back and looked up into his face—tanned and creased with smile lines.

It felt so good to make him smile. "I love you, Daddy," she said. "I missed you."

It was true; she'd missed him so much. But now, instead of coming to rescue her, he'd come to take her away from the ranch and the island she loved. The unicorns and the people who needed her. It wasn't fair. Twig pushed back the sob that wanted to come out. She could do this. Even this. She was a new Twig. She'd always be a herder in her heart, but she'd always be his daughter too.

"I love you too, Twig. I hear you have a lot to show me."

"You have to meet Mrs. Murley and all the girls, and then the ponies and Wonder Light."

Twig introduced her dad to everyone, and then they headed straight for the stable. Casey tugged on Twig's hand and whispered, "Don't worry. Mr. Murley had Ben take Indy to the hollow for now. The plan's still on."

Twig nodded. Her heart beat even faster, thinking of what else she had to show Daddy.

•••

Twig leap-galloped through the pasture, away from the others, then came bounding back. With a gentle nudge, she sent Wonder flying, soaring through the sunshine, bright and beautiful and white as the clouds in the sky. She saw Daddy's smile of amazement, of pride, and her heart soared even higher.

Twig saw Ben approaching, coming up the driveway as though he were just an ordinary boy.

Twig dismounted and went to help Mr. Murley introduce Ben, merely as his nephew and Twig's friend—for now.

"Ben's an even better rider than me," Twig said.

"You should see them ride together!" said Janessa.

"Call Indy," Taylor told Ben.

Ben nodded. He whistled for Indy, just like they'd planned. Twig couldn't ask Daddy to let her stay, but she could show him who she was. Indy bounded to Ben, and Ben ran alongside him and mounted in mid-leap. Twig mounted Wonder and whispered for her to go, to jump, to fly. The unicorns arched through the air together as their horns extended, spiraling, undeniably sharp and bright.

Twig heard Daddy cry out, "Twig!" Her name came out half-choked.

She slowed Wonder and trotted to her dad.

"Is that—is that a…"

Casey slipped her hand around Daddy's. "It's a unicorn, Mr. Tupper. It really is."

"Don't worry," Janessa said. "Twig and Ben are great riders, and Indy and Wonder won't hurt you."

Twig and Ben turned their unicorns out in the pasture, and Mrs. Murley suggested they take her dad, still shaken from what he'd witnessed, inside to talk.

They gathered around the table, and Twig set her latest drawing in front of her dad. "This is all of us, in Terracornus, the land of the unicorns."

He shook his head. His hand shook too as he carefully pulled the drawing closer. He was going to freak out. He was going to make her leave right now. Maybe even tell the authorities, and then all the other girls would have to leave too.

But he reached out and covered Twig's hand with his. "Tell me about it," he said softly. "Tell me all about it."

Across the table, Ben smiled with relief. Twig smiled back.

"Casey tells it best," she said.

"Yes!" all the others said. "Tell him about Terracornus, Casey."

Casey blushed a little. Then she cupped her chin in her hands and leaned over the table. "They said this island was haunted by ghost horses. The people who came here seen something, but that wasn't what they seen. The white creatures moving in the mist—they were unicorns!"

After more stories than Twig could count, and questions and trips to fetch Ben's map and much flipping through Twig's sketchbooks, a visit from Emmie, and four rounds of hot chocolate, Daddy tipped his chair back. He ran his hand over his freshly cut hair.

"It's real."

Twig nodded. "It's real, all of it. The drawings, the stories Casey told you. It's all real."

Daddy turned to the Murleys. They nodded. He blinked at Ben. "You're a prince of this—Terracornus?"

"Yes, sir. Westland, actually."

"His brother, Griffin, is going to be king," Regina said dreamily.

"I knew you were fighting a battle of your own over here,

Twig, but I never dreamed…" Daddy shook his head. He slipped an arm around Twig. "I don't understand all of this, but…I'm proud of you. I wish I had more time with you. I have six months at home, and then I have to leave again for some training."

"Can't you get out?" Mandy said. "Can't you quit?"

"It's what I do."

Twig squeezed Daddy back. She hated it, but she understood.

"Mr. Tupper," Ben said, "Twig saved this island. She saved Indy. She saved me. It's too much to ask—I know it—but I need her. The island needs her."

"Ben," Mr. Murley admonished softly.

"I'm sorry," Ben said.

Twig's dad gave him a nod.

"If you stayed, what would you do?" he asked Twig.

"Save the unicorns. All of us. Together."

•••

Casey stood on the purple throw rug between her bed and Twig's, clutching her old doll to her chest, shaking with silent tears.

Twig yanked the huge gray suitcase Keely had sent her to Lonehorn Island with out of the closet. She hefted it onto her bed and unzipped it.

Daddy came and stood in the open doorway. Casey rubbed at her tears, then ducked under his arm and out the door.

"That's an awfully big suitcase." He went to the closet and rummaged around. He tossed a pair of Twig's shoes aside and held up a small duffel bag. "How about something like this?"

"That's Casey's." Twig sniffed. "But there's no way I'll fit all my things in there anyway."

"I don't think you're going to need *all* your things."

Twig turned her back on the suitcase and looked at her dad.

"Being a soldier…it's what I do. And this…" He gestured at the drawings of ponies and unicorns dancing all over her walls, then out the window at the ranch. "This is what you do, Twig."

"What are you saying?"

"I want you to come back with me. Spend a couple months with Keely and the kids. And then I'll bring you back here."

"Are you sure?"

"You can't leave your Wonder Light. You can't leave that Casey girl who tells all the stories. You can't leave Ben. And you can't leave being a unicorn herder. We could give it a try and—"

Twig threw her arms around him. "Thank you, Daddy. Thank you!"

Footsteps pattered into the room, and a pair of smaller arms wrapped around Daddy's waist. "Thank you, Mr. Tupper!"

Daddy scooped Casey up. "You just make sure our Twig doesn't get into too much trouble."

Casey's smile disappeared. "I'm no good at that, Mr. Tupper."

"Well then, I guess you'll have some more good stories to tell me next time."

The smile was back. "I will for sure. I'm going help Twig, and she's going to help me be a unicorn rider one of these days."

Daddy brushed Twig's hair back. He looked right into her eyes. "That's my Twig," he said, just as though she were sprouting leaves of pure gold.

Epilogue

THE SWEEPING CEDAR BOUGHS around the passage tree ripped open, and a blur of white, red, and gold charged through. Indy reared at the strange mare plunging into the circle of mist, and Ben struggled to settle him. The mare's quicksilver eyes gleamed with eagerness for the Earth Land. It was the first time she'd set foot in this world.

"This is Night Spark," Griffin said once he had her under control.

"She is magnificent," Ben said. She was nearly as tall as Indy, gleaming white, with a cream-colored mane and a buttery stripe around her horn. It gave her a gilded look, as though she were meant to be royalty.

Griffin ran his hand down the side of her neck. "Returning her to Mother was one of the hardest things I've ever done. She was just learning how to be free. Mother tried to get me to tell her where I kept the others, but I wouldn't do it." He gave Ben an apologetic smile. "She didn't haul me to the dungeon. She's afraid now, of looking like a tyrant."

"Lucky for you."

Griffin shrugged. "Lucky for the unicorns."

"She let you take Night Spark out after you gave her back?"

"Oh no. She told me to take her for good. She thinks she's ruined."

"Ruined!"

Griffin grinned. "Unruly. Uninterested in the arena."

Indy walked a slow circle around Night Spark, checking her out. The unicorns sniffed each other. After a minute, they settled nose beside nose, horns to the side, making soft, breathy sounds. Almost as if they were whispering in each other's ears.

"Well…" Ben said, "are you ready?"

"Ready enough."

Darian's grave was marked with a pile of stones, each chosen with care and carried from the beach. The smoothest, the whitest Ben could find.

Ben read a passage from the Bible, and Griffin stood beside him, head bowed. Griffin dropped to his knees in the dirt, hands on the stones. Ben tucked the Bible back into the pouch at his hip and knelt next to his brother. Indy whickered softly. He bent down and nuzzled Ben's cheek. Ben put one hand on Griffin's back. With the other, he cupped Indy's velvety muzzle. Night Spark edged close to Griffin, making quiet, encouraging sounds.

Griffin looked at Ben. He took an object out of his pocket—the unicorn whistle Ben had refused to take in the Death Swamp.

Ben thought he was going to offer it to him again, but instead he said, "This seems as good a place as any to bury it."

They buried the unicorn whistle together, under the white stones. After a while, Griffin sat back and wiped the tears from his face. He pulled another instrument out of his pocket.

"Don't worry," he said. "This one's just a flute." He sat back and began to play.

Ben closed his eyes and listened, lost in the mixture of memory, of the familiarity of the song, and of the strangeness of being so close to his brother. Lost in the unanswered questions about what he was going to do, where he was going to stay, what his future was going to be. Ahead of him was the hollow, where Indy was waiting with Griffin's unicorn. Behind him was the ranch, where everyone was waiting for Twig to come back, trying to figure out how to be Island Ranch without her.

The final note drifted away, and Griffin lowered the flute.

Ben didn't know what he was going to do or where he was going to go tomorrow, but he knew what he needed to do today. He put a hand on Griffin's arm. "Let's go to the hollow and get something to eat."

Griffin just stared at Ben for a moment. He wasn't going to

come. What had he been thinking? The old, familiar resentment stirred in Ben.

But then Griffin spoke. His voice cracked with emotion. "Would you really take me there?"

Ben nodded slowly. "This is where Father died. You should see where he lived. Besides, I have Father's old flute there. I never really used it, but…you could teach me how to play, I think."

"I'm going to be a prince *and* a herder," Griffin said. "I was hoping you could help me with that."

The wind whipped Indy's mane and Night Spark's too. The island's mist encircled them, embracing them with its wildness, its mystery. The only sons of the great Darian rode through the twilight shadows of Lonehorn Island—one clad in woodland green, the other trimmed in royal red and gold.

Acknowledgments

Who am I, that the God of the universe is by my side? But He is, always. I'd like to thank every friend and family member who's reminded me of that. Your smiles are his smiles. Your hugs are his arms around me, whether we're joined in laughter or in aching hearts.

I'd also like to thank Aubrey Poole and the Sourcebooks team, as well as all the readers, booksellers, teachers, and librarians who champion my books. I'm so grateful for you all!

About the Author

R.R. Russell lives with her family in the Pacific Northwest. She grew up traveling the world as an army brat and now travels the country as a coach with a nonprofit judo club. She loves to read and draw, and like Twig, once spent a lot of time sketching unicorns. Visit her website at RRRussellauthor.com.

Wonder Light

Book 1 of the
Unicorns of the Mist series

R.R. Russell

Deep in the heart of a mist-shrouded island,
an impossible secret is about to be discovered.

There in the hay—a bleating little scrap of moonbeam. A silver-white filly with cloven hooves and a tiny, spiraling horn.

A baby unicorn.

Now Twig knows what secret is hiding in the island's mist: the last free unicorn herd. And a mysterious boy named Ben who insists that this impossible creature is now Twig's to care for. That she needs Twig's love and protection. Because there's something out there in the deep, dense shadows that's hunting for them…

To learn more
about the

Unicorns of
the Mist

visit
UnicornsOfTheMist.com